Winner Books are produced by Victor Books and are designed to entertain and instruct young readers in Christian principles. Each book has been approved by specialists in Christian education and children's literature. These books uphold the teachings and principles of the Bible.

Other Winner Books you will enjoy:

Sarah and the Magic Twenty-fifth, by Margaret Epp
Sarah and the Pelican, by Margaret Epp
Sarah and the Lost Friendship, by Margaret Epp
Sarah and the Mystery of the Hidden Boy, by Margaret Epp
Sarah and the Darnley Boys, by Margaret Epp
The Hairy Brown Angel and Other Animal Tails, edited by Grace Fox Anderson
The Peanut Butter Hamster and Other Animal Tails, edited by Grace Fox Anderson
Danger on the Alaskan Trail (three mysteries)
Gopher Hole Treasure Hunt, by Ralph Bartholomew
Patches, by Edith Buck
The Taming of Cheetah, by Lee Roddy
Ted and the Secret Club, by Bernard Palmer
The Mystery Man of Horseshoe Bend, by Linda Boorman
The Giant Trunk Mystery, by Linda Boorman
The Drugstore Bandit of Horseshoe Bend by Linda Boorman
Colby Moves West, by Sharon Miller

EDITH VIRGINIA BUCK grew up in Fairbanks, Alaska and, as a bride, lived right on the new Alcan Highway. She received a B.S. in music from New York University and studied special education and music education at the University of Washington. Circumstances and interest in "special" children led her into teaching and coordinating special education. A widow, she has worked with children of all ages in public school, church, and camps and has three married daughters. All of her writing has centered around children and family relationships.

TREASURE
IN GOLDEN
CANYON

EDITH BUCK

Illustrated by
Darwin Dunham

A WINNER BOOK

VICTOR
BOOKS a division of SP Publications, Inc.
WHEATON. ILLINOIS 60187

Offices also in
Whitby, Ontario, Canada
Amersham-on-the-Hill, Bucks, England

Library of Congress Catalog Card Number: 82-62082
ISBN: 0-88207-494-6

VICTOR BOOKS
A division of SP Publications, Inc.
P. O. Box 1825 • Wheaton, Illinois 60187

Contents

1   Sam   **7**

2   Treasure in a Box   **14**

3   The Picnic   **23**

4   Does Anybody Love Me?   **33**

5   Fire!   **42**

6   Trapped!   **49**

7   At Home with the Duffeys   **62**

8   Sam Learns a Lesson   **74**

9   Golden Canyon   **86**

10   Quite a Find   **100**

11   Sam Goes Home   **110**

      Glossary   **117**

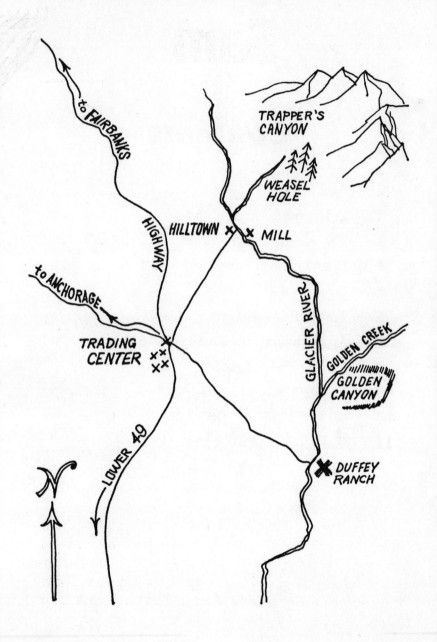

Sam

1

The Glacier River that ran past the Duffey ranch was almost dry. Peter Duffey knew the river well. He had lived near the Nutzetin Mountains in Alaska and the Glacier River for most of his life.

Peter squatted on a rock in the middle of the river. He picked up one rock and then another to look at the odd shapes.

"Peter!" His mother called from the kitchen door.

"Over here, Mom," he answered. He slipped some choice rocks into his pocket.

"Dad's ready to go. Come on!"

Peter jumped from the rock to the riverbank and ran toward the house. The sleeping sled dogs woke up as he raced by their kennels. He was always eager to go to the Trading Center at the Alcan Highway junction. Today was Peter's first trip there since he had come back from

Fairbanks. He could hardly wait to see his old friends at the Center. Mr. Hunter owned the general store. Mrs. Hunter always gave Peter extra jelly beans when he asked for a pound. There was J.D. at the service station and Maria at the soda shop. Were they all still there? Would they remember him?

"Bye, Mom," Peter waved. "We'll be home by 5 at the latest, won't we Dad?"

"We'll try," said his dad. The jeep growled into action. "Bye, Hon," he called to his wife. "I've got your list right here," and he patted his shirt pocket.

Alice Duffey watched as the two drove out of the gate. Then she went back into the kitchen where jam was simmering on the stove.

The little jeep rattled over the gravel road, spreading dust over the roadside bushes and trees. The purple fireweed* was blooming early. It blended in with the goldenrod* flowers. The birch* and aspen* trees danced in the light breeze. A tiny chipmunk scurried across the road.

Peter rode silently, watching every bush and tree. It all looked so familiar. The old tree with an eagle's nest on top stood where it always had. The old tumble-down trapper's cabin was still tumbling down in the exact same place. Peter wondered if the soaring hawk was the same one he had seen the last time they'd gone to the Trading Center. The jeep rounded the last curve and crossed the bridge. Peter yelled, "There it is!" He pointed to the Trading Center on the north bank of the river. Several cars were parked at Mr. Hunter's store, and Peter

*You can find an explanation of the starred words in the Glossary on pages 117-120.

counted three trucks at the service station.

"They're busy today," said Peter.

"They're always busy," answered his dad. He parked the jeep against the porch of the store. Around the corner two saddled horses stood roped to the porch railing. They grazed on the tall grass beside the store.

"Hey, look," said Peter, pointing to the horses. "Aren't they beauties? Look at that little one!" He whistled softly. To have a horse of his own was his dream.

"They're from Milltown," said his dad. Milltown was a small logging town with a lumber mill up the river from the ranch. Peter had gone there at times with his mom and dad. There was no road from the Duffey ranch to Milltown, so they always drove along the winding riverbank in the jeep. The trip to Milltown took about two hours.

There were several people in the store. Two women were half hidden among the heavy jackets and mukluks* in the back. Another woman looked at cloth while her husband filled a sack with nails. Peter saw Mr. Hunter behind the jewelry counter. He was talking to a boy, but when he saw Peter he stopped.

"Pete! Peter Duffey!" Mr. Hunter threw up his hands in surprise. "It's great to see you! How you've grown! Hey, you're almost as tall as that dad of yours! Be with you in a minute." Mr. Hunter turned his attention back to the boy.

"Take your time, Bill," said Jack Duffey. "No great hurry here." Peter's father walked to the shelves of food and picked up a sack of flour and then a sack of sugar.

Peter studied the boy who was talking to Mr. Hunter. He had blond hair and was very thin. He stood a bit taller than Peter. He held something that he was showing to Mr. Hunter. Peter moved closer. The boy laid down some small pieces of ivory on the counter. Peter stretched his neck to get a better look. He could see tiny pictures on the ivory pieces.

Mr. Hunter picked up one small piece and then another, and stared at them closely. "Very nice, Sam." He laid down the first two pieces and picked up what looked like a bracelet. He peered at the blond boy over the top of his glasses. "Did you do all of these?"

Sam swallowed hard. "Y-yes, sir, I did them. All by myself."

"Tell you what. I'll take all of them for $15."

"F-for f-fifteen dollars? Fifteen dollars?"

"What's the matter? Isn't that enough?"

"Oh yes, I'll take it, Mr. Hunter. Fifteen dollars— that's a lot of money. That's great. Thanks, thanks a lot."

Peter glanced from the boy's shining eyes to the jewelry and back again to the boy. He felt excited too as Mr. Hunter counted the money out into the boy's hand. Peter stepped closer to the counter and picked up one of the pins. It was round with a picture of a seal carved on it in fine black lines. The other had a sunburst. The bracelet was made of squares of ivory fastened together. Each square had a tiny flower carved on it.

A man and woman with two girls had come into the store. They too were interested in what Sam had.

Peter could keep quiet no longer. "You made these? Really?"

"How do you do it?" Peter had seen scrimshaw* before. He was surprised to find a boy his own age who could do it and sell it.

Sam glanced at Mr. Hunter as if for help. The storekeeper came and stood beside the boys. "Come on, Sam," he said, "take Peter out on the porch and get acquainted. Show him how you do scrimshaw. He'd like to know, wouldn't you, Pete? Pete, I want to have a long talk with you soon. I want to hear all about your school in Fairbanks."

The man put an arm around Sam's shoulders and gently led him to the door. Sam walked in an awkward way, dragging one foot as he went. One arm dangled at his side. The two girls stared at Sam. "Look at him," whispered one to the other. Then they both giggled.

Peter was glad when they got to the porch and sat down. Now he wouldn't have to see how Sam walked—but there was still Sam's limp arm. Peter wondered what to say.

Before Peter could speak, Sam took a piece of ivory and a nail out of his pocket. He put the ivory in his almost useless left hand. Then he rested his arm on the porch railing. He began to scratch a design on the ivory with the nail. "Like this," he said.

Silently Sam etched* while Peter watched. Slowly a tiny flower began to take shape. Sam stopped to blow away the fine dust on the ivory. "Do you live around here?" Peter asked.

"In Milltown," Sam said. He started scratching on the ivory again. "Where do you live?"

"On the Duffey ranch. I'm Peter—Peter Duffey."

"Oh," a smile broke on Sam's face. "I know where the Duffey ranch is. It's down the river from Milltown. Do you come to the Trading Center often?"

"My dad and I come here every week or so," answered Peter. "My mom usually comes too."

Sam frowned. "My mom died when I was born." He bent his head to work on the ivory again.

"Pete, ready to go?" Peter's father asked. He had his arms full of packages. "Oh, you have a new friend."

"Dad, this is Sam. Come see what he's doing!"

"Glad to know you, Sam." Mr. Duffey walked over to the boys. "Scrimshaw!" he said. "Say, that's pretty nice."

"Nothin' much," said Sam. He rubbed the ivory on the leg of his pants.

"It will be." Peter was feeling proud for Sam. "He just sold some scrimshaw to Mr. Hunter for $15!"

"Is that right! Say, how would you two like a soda? Sam, can you come with Peter and me to get one before we head for home?"

Sam looked up with a smile on his face. He started to answer, then he frowned. "My brother—"

Peter watched a tall young man, blond like Sam, climb over the porch railing. He came toward the three.

"Sam, did you get your money? You'd better let me carry it." He held out his hand.

Sam reached into his pocket and pulled out the bills

Mr. Hunter had given him. "Fifteen," he said as he laid them in his brother's hand.

"Is that all?"

"Fifteen," repeated Sam.

Peter looked from Sam to his brother. "I saw Mr. Hunter—" he began.

His father put his hand on Peter's shoulder. "We would like for Sam to have a soda with us."

"Sam has to come with me right away." The older boy stared at Sam.

Sam stood up and put the ivory and nail in his pocket. Slowly he made his way across the porch. Peter felt embarrassed.

"We'll come see you sometime, Sam. Won't we, Dad?"

"We sure will! Tell you what, Sam. What if we take you on a picnic two weeks from today? Will he be able to go?" Jack Duffey looked at the older boy.

"Sure, if you really want to take him. I'll tell Dad." Then he called out, "Hurry up, Sam!" He led the way to the two horses tied in the grass.

Sam mounted his horse with his brother's help. Without looking at Peter, he rode after his brother down the narrow trail that led to Milltown.

"Look at them go!" exclaimed Peter. "Sure wish I had a horse—one just like Sam's."

Treasure in a Box

2

"But Mom," Peter helped himself to more potatoes, "he could hardly walk. He had to drag one foot behind him. And his left arm was so limp! But he could hold the ivory in his hand. He sure can do scrimshaw and ride a horse!"

"Perhaps he has cerebral palsy*," said Mrs. Duffey.

"Like Freddy! I'll bet he's like Freddy!"

"And who is Freddy?" Peter's father asked.

"He's a kid at school, like Sam only worse."

"Now really, Peter," his mother smiled. "First you say Sam is like Freddy, and then Freddy is like Sam only worse! Would you explain that please?"

"Freddy has C.P. That's what everybody calls it—and I'll bet they mean cerebral palsy. It means that something's wrong with the part of his brain that makes his muscles work. Freddy's like Sam 'cause Sam has C.P.

too—if that's what he has. Only Freddy's got it a lot worse."

"You're still not very clear, Son," said his father. "How is Freddy worse?"

"Freddy has to stay in a wheelchair. He can't walk and I guess he never will." Peter was quiet for a few seconds, remembering Freddy. "And—and his arms go like this." He flung his arms around as though he could not control them.

"Peter!" said his mother.

"That's really the way his arms go, Mom. He can't help it. He's a good kid though."

"A 'good kid'?" repeated his dad.

"Yeah, everybody likes him."

"Does Freddy go to school with the rest of the boys and girls?"

"Sure. He's right in class with us. A lady does his writing for him. He tells her his spelling and math answers and all the things we have to write. If he makes a mistake—tough. She just writes it down the way he says it. She even has to help him eat."

"Poor boy," Alice looked at her own son.

"He's OK," said Peter. "The kids all take turns pushing him around in his wheelchair. He laughs a lot."

Probably cries a lot too, thought Peter's mother. Aloud she said, "Sam isn't as crippled as Freddy, then."

"No, but he is crippled. Are we really taking him on a picnic? How will we find him? We don't even know his last name!"

"That's the date we made," said his father. "We'll go to

Milltown and ask for a boy called Sam. Milltown isn't that big. We'll find him. Now finish your dinner."

As the sun dipped low in the sky, the three Duffeys sat around the dining table. It was the time of the midnight sun, and the nights did not get completely dark. The sun dipped just below the horizon for about three hours, but it still gave the sky a dusky light. It was hard for a boy to know just when it was bedtime unless, of course, he was told.

The dinner dishes had been washed and put away. Peter and his parents played catch until they were tired. Then the family gathered again around the table with their Bibles.

Jack Duffey read from Psalm 139. "I will give thanks to Thee, for I am fearfully and wonderfully made; wonderful are Thy works, and my soul knows it very well."

"Dad," Peter looked up at his father who stopped reading. "Why is Sam the way he is? And Freddy? Why didn't God let them be like me and the rest of the kids?"

"That's a hard question to answer, Son. We can't understand God's ways. He made us the way we are for His own reasons. God wants us to honor Him with the bodies we have—no matter what shape or color or size they are. We should pray that both Sam and Freddy know Jesus Christ as their Saviour. Then He will help them live the way He wants them to live."

"It doesn't seem fair," protested Peter.

"We can't judge God, Pete," said his mother. "We can only trust Him. Maybe He wants to work through us in those boys' lives."

Peter was silent as his father read from the Bible again. When it was his turn to pray, he asked, "Dear God, help me to be a good friend to Sam and to Freddy, if I ever see him again. Help me to tell Sam about You when we go on our picnic. In Jesus' name. Amen."

* * *

Peter was up early the next morning. After breakfast, he walked out toward the pasture. The grass was turning yellow and brown because there had been no rain. But the cattle and sheep didn't seem to mind.

"If it doesn't rain soon we'll have to hay the animals," his father had said.

Old Nell, the slowpoke farm horse, stood under a tree swishing flies with her tail. Peter walked up to her quietly.

"Nice Nellie," he said and rubbed her velvet nose. "Nice ol' girl. Will you let me ride you?" He looked for a way to climb on her bare back. If he could get out on the branch Nell was standing under, he could drop onto her back.

Quickly Peter climbed the tree trunk and worked his way out on the branch. Bit by bit, the branch bent under his weight. Just as he was over his target, the branch broke and the noise scared Nell. As fast as she could, Nell moved out from under the tree. Peter slid to the ground with a thud.

He sat in the grass, thinking of another way to ride Nell. He took hold of her mane and led her over to a stile* that had been built over the fence. The horse stood still while Peter climbed the stile. After three tries he swung one leg across Old Nell's broad back. Hanging on to her mane and neck, he finally balanced himself and sat up.

"Whoopee, I made it! C'mon ol' girl, let's go!" He dug his heels into her flanks. Old Nell looked at the boy over her shoulder and swished her tail. She headed slowly down the pasture to where Peter's dad was mending the fence.

"Well, where do you think you're off to?" said Jack Duffey, laughing.

"Dad, why can't I have a real horse?"

"Nell *is* a real horse—mane, tail, eyes, ears."

"Oh, Dad! She won't run! She's too old."

"It takes a lot of money to keep a horse, Pete. Think how much it would cost to feed another one during the winter."

"But you feed Nell."

"Nell earns her feed," answered his dad. "She's not much for riding, but she's still a good plow horse and she hauls logs. There's a big difference between a work horse and a riding horse."

"I want a horse to ride. That's really what they're for!"

"Pete, we just can't afford one now. Maybe someday." Peter knew from his father's tone of voice that he had better keep quiet. Old Nell had found a patch of clover to nibble on. Peter slid out of the saddle and stood beside his father.

"Here, hold this. You're old enough to learn to stretch fence wire."

Peter had an idea. "If I work hard, maybe I could earn a horse's keep. Even buy my own horse."

"Pull it tighter," was his dad's reply.

The sun rose high in the clear sky and Peter pulled wire, handed his father staples, then pulled wire again.

"Can we quit now?" Peter asked. It seemed like they had been working on the fence for hours.

"We'll quit at lunchtime," his father answered.

When they heard the call for lunch, a tired and hungry boy walked to the house beside his father.

After lunch Peter started for his room, but he stopped. "Is there anything else you want me to do this afternoon, Dad?"

"You forgot the eggs this morning," reminded his mother.

"After that, bring in some more wood," added his dad. "I'm going to work on the tractor."

Peter raced to the chicken house. He reached into the warm nests and found the freshly laid eggs. He talked to the hens that were scratching in the dust and to the proud rooster that was strutting up and down.

"Oh, 'cluck, cluck' yourself" he said as he closed the chicken-yard gate behind him.

"Back so soon? That was fast?" His mother smiled at him.

"Yes'm," said Peter. Again he headed for his room. But first he asked, "Anything else?"

"You can clean the eggs later," his mother said as she shook her head. She knew Peter had something else on his mind. "I'll set them on the porch for now. You can

take care of them while I'm cooking dinner."

With some time to himself, Peter went into his bedroom. He pulled out the box of treasures he kept hidden under his bed. There were rocks from the riverbed, pieces of wood, an old silver belt buckle, some pieces of thick blue glass, marbles, a knife. Finally he found what he was looking for—a flat piece of old ivory. A trapper who lived back in Golden Canyon had given this to his father and his father had given it to him.

Peter moved over to the window to see the ivory better. He rubbed it on his shirt sleeve and studied both sides of it. Then he went out to the toolshed. Taking a sack needle from his father's kit, Peter sat down on the back steps of the house.

Carefully he tried to scratch the hard yellow ivory with the sharp needle. The needle slipped and stuck his hand.

"Ow!" Peter dropped the ivory and sucked the tiny dot of blood. He picked up the ivory and tried again. Nothing happened. Again he tried and again. At last a thin jagged line showed where the needle had wobbled across.

His mother came out of the kitchen and sat down beside him. "What are you doing?"

"Oh, nothing!" Peter sounded impatient.

"Well, then, what are you trying to do?"

"Scrimshaw—and I can't do it!"

"Scrimshaw? Here, let me see." Mrs. Duffey took the warm ivory into her own hand. "You made a scratch. That's a start!"

"But it's so hard! The needle keeps slipping. I jabbed myself three times."

"It looks very hard. I'm sure it will take a lot of practice and patience. After all, this is your first try."

"I wonder how Sam learned to do it. You should see what he makes, Mom. It's so easy for him—and he's only got one good arm!" After a few minutes, Peter spoke again. "I wonder why his brother's so mean to him."

"You don't know that he's mean, Peter. Maybe he was in a hurry to get home."

"He took all of Sam's money."

"Fifteen dollars is a lot of money for a boy to carry. His brother was probably making sure that Sam didn't lose it."

"Oh, Mom!" Peter rested his head against his mother's shoulder. "You always make excuses for everybody."

"It's not fair to judge other people, Pete. If you find fault with other people for things they do, it may mean you do the same thing."

"I haven't got a brother to be mean to," muttered Peter. He tried another scratch on the ivory and stabbed his hand again.

Mrs. Duffey slapped at a mosquito on her arm. She stood to go into the kitchen and looked across the fields. "We *do* need some rain. I don't know when it's been so dry. Don't forget to clean the eggs."

The Picnic

3

The night before the picnic, Peter stayed up to work on his ivory. He had wanted to finish it—to show both Sam and his parents that he could do scrimshaw too. But the yellow ivory kept slipping out of his hand as if it were alive. With a sigh, Peter finally gave up and started to bed.

He walked through the kitchen and spotted the covered cake dish. Surely there was some icing that had dripped onto the plate that he could scoop off with his finger. He was about to pick up the cover of the dish when a sleepy voice from his parents' room called, "Peter! Go to bed right now!"

Peter left the cake dish alone. How could his mother always know what he was doing even when she was supposed to be asleep?

When he woke in the morning, Peter jumped out of

bed to get an early start. The chickens and pigs needed food and water. And the empty woodbox had to be filled once again.

"Breakfast!" his mother called. Peter dumped his last armload of wood into the box.

"When can we leave, Dad?" he asked as they sat down to eat.

"As soon as we're ready. Mother has the lunch to pack and the dishes have to be washed. I'll load the jeep while you help Mom. OK?"

Peter picked up his spoon and aimed at his bowl of steaming oatmeal. "Peter!" He put his spoon down and bowed his head.

"I'm sorry," he whispered. How could he have forgotten? Shame burned on his cheeks.

"Our Father," began Mr. Duffey, "thank You for seeing us safely through another night. We thank You for Your love and care for us. Bless this food to our bodies' use and us to Thy service. In Jesus' name. Amen."

Peter forced himself to eat slowly. After they had eaten, his father read from John chapter 15. "This is My commandment, that you love one another, just as I have loved you. Greater love has no one than this, that one lay down his life for his friends."

Jesus had laid down His life, Peter knew. Would he himself ever be called on to prove his love for anyone that way? He bowed his head again as his mother prayed, "We ask, Lord, for a safe trip to Milltown and a good day with young Sam. May we show him Your love."

The drive to Milltown was pleasant. Peter, sitting on a

box, leaned over the back of the seat between his parents so he could talk to them.

"What if we were missionaries going into a jungle!" he said.

"Aren't you a missionary going to Milltown?" asked his mother.

"I don't know. Am I?"

"Of course, we all are. We want to tell Sam about the Lord, if He opens the way." After a pause she said, "My goodness, look how low the river is—even up here!"

"Hey, Dad, did you put in the fishing poles?"

"I put them in alright, but I don't think we'll use them. Look over there where you went finishing once."

Peter looked at the big rock under the aspen tree. On other days, that spot was full of silver grayling. Now the rock stood out of the water and was dry.

Peter whistled. "Let's go look, Dad."

"Look at what?" asked his father. "There's nothing there!"

But even as he spoke, he brought the jeep to a stop. Peter jumped out and ran to the big rock. Two or three little puddles of water lay where the pool should have been. Bits of algae clung to the pebbles.

"No fish here today," said Jack Duffey. "Maybe farther up where the Golden River runs into this one."

But every pool was shallow. The grass along the river was dry and rustled as the jeep passed over it.

One hour, two hours passed. Then Peter shouted, "I see it!" as they rounded a curve. "There's the sawmill and there's Milltown!"

Men unloaded logs from big trucks. Other logs were stacked into piles, ready to be cut for lumber. Sawdust made a golden cloud in the air and a sweet-smelling mountain of it grew where it fell from the blower.

"Hmm. Look how low the water is in the mill pond," Jack Duffey said.

They crossed the wooden bridge and drove past rows of dog kennels. Small wooden houses lined both sides of the narrow street.

Curious children stopped their play as the jeep drove by. The Duffeys parked in front of a small wooden building with a big yellow GROCERIES sign nailed over the door.

"Which house do you suppose is Sam's?" asked Peter.

"I'll check in here," said his dad.

After getting directions, Jack Duffey climbed back into the jeep. He made one right-hand turn, then pulled up in front of the second house on the right.

Sam's house was small, wooden, and neatly painted. A narrow path led from the street to the porch. Brightly colored hollyhocks* bloomed near the house. A ring of velvety pansies* peeked out from an old tire made into a flower bed.

In back of the house were the usual dog kennels. In a small pasture behind the house were two horses. Peter recognized them as the same horses Sam and his brother had ridden from the Trading Center.

Sam's brother came out of the house. Jack got out and walked toward him.

"Jack Duffey," he said as he held out his hand to the

boy. "We met at the Trading Center, but I don't know your name."

"I'm Caleb—Caleb Sealth." The young man shook Jack's hand.

"This is Mrs. Duffey," Jack motioned to Alice in the jeep, "and Peter. We've come to take Sam on that picnic."

"Sam, hurry up!" Caleb called into the house. "The Duffeys are ready to go."

Slowly Sam came on to the porch. He smiled shyly at Jack who said, "Hi, Sam. Ready to go? See you later," Peter's father said to Caleb. "We'll be on Trapper Canyon Road."

Peter and Sam sat on the floor of the jeep. Soon they were talking like best buddies.

Peter pulled his piece of ivory out of his pocket and showed it to Sam. Sam looked at it closely and laughed. "You don't know how," he said. "You didn't polish it first." Sam handed it back.

Peter never dreamed that Sam would laugh at him. It hurt—on the inside where no one could see. He dropped the ivory back into his pocket.

The road grew rougher as it wound back into the woods and climbed into the foothills. Soon they came to the clearing that lay about a mile behind the mill. The smokestack and blower could barely be seen through the trees.

With a jump, Peter was out of the jeep. Then he remembered to wait for Sam, who climbed out slowly. Together the boys explored the picnic spot. A large flat rock covered with pinecone bits was under a tall tree. "Hey Mom, here's a table," said Peter. He brushed off the pieces of pinecone and needles.

"Don't go far, boys," warned Peter's mother. "We'll be eating soon."

The two were already walking toward the edge of the clearing behind the flat rock. "Look at those funny rocks over there!" Peter pointed at two tall rocks that leaned toward each other. Stepping over old logs and small stones, the boys went to explore. A stony ledge, half-covered with grass and brush, stuck out from under the tall rocks. Neither boy saw the grass-covered pit under the ledge until it was too late. Peter's feet went out from under him and he slid down the gravel slope. Sam slid too, then rolled over and over until he stopped against a log.

The pit was not much deeper than the boys were tall. Its bottom was sandy and several old logs lay there crisscross on top of each other.

"Hey, how about that!" exclaimed Peter.

"Whew!" said Sam, rolling over so he could push himself up.

"This'd be a great hide out!" said Peter.

"Hideout? What from?"

"Oh, I don't know. From robbers—or hoodlums. Just anything you'd want to hide from."

"That's what he must think," said Sam, pointing to a log.

"What is it?"

"See that knot hole? Look at what's peeking out of it!"

"Now I see it," Peter said. A furry little head with bright beady eyes hid in the hole. "It's a weasel*, isn't it? Hi, fella." Peter knelt down to get a better look. "He's sure brave. He'd even try to kill an eagle, if it tried to catch him. I wouldn't want him getting hold of my finger! Imagine being able to crawl through a knot hole. He must have his home in that log."

Sam pressed his ear against the log. "He has. I can hear babies in there. Wish I could see them."

"We'll have to call this place Weasel Hole," said Peter.

"Pete! Sam! Where are you?"

"Over here, Dad," answered Peter, "down here in Weasel Hole. Watch out so you don't slide in too."

"Looks like somebody started to dig a gravel pit once," Pete's dad peered through the grass at the boys.

"Come on, now. Mother's got everything ready." Leaning down, Jack helped Sam out of the pit. But Peter scrambled up alone.

The two boys sat side by side on a log with their plates of food on their laps. Before they ate, Mr. Duffey said a short prayer. After Sam tasted the fried chicken he said, "When we lived in Tanana our next-door neighbor told me about Jesus. She said He loves everybody, even me."

"That's right," agreed Peter. "He loves us and you—I mean, you and us—so He died for us." Peter remembered the Bible verses he had heard that morning. "Nobody has greater love than to give his life for his friends. Jesus gave His life for us," explained Peter.

Just then Sam's brother rode up on his horse.

"Sam, are you giving these people any trouble?" Caleb looked down at his brother.

"He's great," said Jack. "Are you hungry, Caleb?"

"The cake sure looks good," Caleb said as he slid from his horse.

Sam watched his brother. "Are you sure you're having a good time?" asked Caleb again. His mouth was full of chocolate cake.

Peter walked over to the horse that nibbled the grass. The horse lifted his head. He was so small and graceful compared to Old Nell! Gently Peter rubbed the horse's soft nose.

"Would you like to ride him?" Caleb asked Peter. "I don't have to be at the mill for 10 minutes yet."

"Ride him? Sure! Can I?" Peter knew this was the chance of a lifetime. Now he could show his dad that he could ride a *real* horse.

Caleb held the horse's bridle* with one hand and boosted Peter up with the other. Caleb handed him the reins.

"Go slow, Prince," Caleb told the horse.

Prince did go slowly at first. Then a toad jumped right under his nose. The startled horse gave a low snort and took off at top speed.

Peter tried to stay in the saddle, but his legs were too short to reach the stirrups. After three hard bounces, he flew through the air and landed in a patch of fireweed.

Jack, seeing his boy was not hurt, laughed at the surprised look on Peter's face. Caleb laughed too.

"Peter!" his mother cried. Then she began to laugh.

"He's OK, Alice. He's just dazed," Jack Duffey said.

Peter stood up slowly and walked away. One hand was on his sore seat. With the other hand, he wiped away a tear before anyone could see.

Does Anyone Love Me?

4

"Peter, why don't you and Sam play catch while I pack up the lunch things?" his mother asked.

Peter shook his head.

"Oh, come now, you're not hurt!" protested his mother.

"I don't want to play catch."

"Sam and I'll play," Peter's dad said. "Come on, Sam." He tossed the ball to the boy. Sam grinned as he caught it with his right hand.

The heavy jackets felt good as everyone climbed into the jeep. Peter watched the picnic spot with the strange rocks and Weasel Hole fade out of sight. Sam asked, "Are you hurt?"

Peter shook his head. How could he tell Sam of his *real* hurt?

"You polish your ivory. The next time I'll show you how to do scrimshaw."

Peter felt his piece of ivory in his pocket. He pulled it out and held it out to Sam. "Here, you take it."

"No, it's yours."

"I don't want it," said Peter. "Here." He tossed the piece to Sam.

When the jeep pulled up to Sam's house, a pickup truck was parked in front. "My dad's home," said Sam as he climbed out of the jeep. "He comes home from the mill when Caleb goes to work. He's asleep by now."

Peter's mother opened the hamper and took out the leftover chicken and cake. "Take the rest of this food for your family."

"Thanks," said Sam, "thanks a lot. It's been a great day. Thanks."

"Thank you for coming, Sam. Someday you'll come to the ranch." Alice Duffey called after him as he went into the house.

Sam watched the jeep drive away. He felt good all over—and tired. Only one thing had cast a shadow over the fun of the day. No, two things.

The first shadow came when Caleb showed up to check on him. Why couldn't Caleb leave him alone? The Duffeys didn't care if Sam was different from other boys. They seemed to like him just the way he was. For once, Sam wanted to feel that he *really* was like other boys—well, almost like them. But Caleb spoiled everything.

Sam made his way to his father's bedroom and peeked inside. In the dim light he could see the big man on the bed. "Sam, is that you?"

"Yes, it's me, Dad," said Sam softly, then backed away from the door. His father worked hard as a foreman at the mill. He worked nights and slept during the day, but Caleb worked from late afternoon until far into the night. Sam would see his dad for an hour or two after his dad woke up and then he would see his brother when he woke up in the morning. It was a lonely life for the boy.

Sam sighed as he went into the kitchen. He wanted to tell his dad about the Duffeys. And he wanted to tell him how Caleb had ruined the picnic. Sam knew what his father would say. "Your brother wanted to make sure you were alright."

As long as Sam could remember, Caleb had been taking care of him. When Caleb wanted to go places, sometimes he had to stay home because of Sam. When Caleb was in a hurry, he had to wait because Sam was so slow. Sam was sure too that when Caleb's friends came to the house, his brother was embarrassed.

Sam took Peter's piece of ivory from his pocket and turned it over and over in his hand. He would make something pretty on it. First he would polish it till it was smooth and shiny. Then he would scratch a picture on it. To make the picture stand out, he would rub black ink over it.

An old Indian had taught Sam to do scrimshaw and the boy had learned quickly. Caleb always liked what he made. Sam worked hard to hear Caleb whistle in delight.

Sam pushed the dirty dishes on the kitchen table to one side, then he sat down to polish the ivory. He worked in silence then said, "There. Isn't it getting nice?" Sam

whispered the words as he began his game of pretending. He imagined his mother was standing at the stove.

She turned and whispered back, "Very beautiful, my
dear."

"What should I make out of this piece?" Sam whispered toward the stove. "What would you like?"

"A pin with a flower etched on it," was the answer he
heard. Then "I love you, Son."

Sam kept his eyes on the ivory. *I love you, Son,* he said
again in his heart. What had Peter said about God and
His Son? "He loved us—you too, Sam." That's what
Peter had said—that Jesus, God's Son, loved him. What
else had Peter said? Sam thought for a minute, then
remembered. Jesus had loved him enough to give His
life for him.

But if Jesus loved him so much, why did He let him be
made with a body that didn't work right? If Jesus really
loved him, wouldn't He have given him two good legs
and two good arms? Sam shook his head. No, Jesus
couldn't have loved *him.* Sam said to himself, *Peter, yes,
and Peter's mom and dad because they knew Him. But
not me—no, Jesus wouldn't have let me be the way I am
if He loved me. Maybe I can do something that will make
Him love me.*

Sam's thought about his mother. "Did you love me like
that, Mother? Did you love me enough to give your life
for me? Maybe because you died, Dad wishes I hadn't
been born—maybe—maybe—you didn't want to be with
me 'cause I'm so crippled."

Jesse Sealth heard Sam whispering in the kitchen. He

knew the game of pretending Sam played, for he had heard him before. Each time he heard it, Jesse felt sad. He remembered Maria . . . she had been small with blue eyes and soft curly hair. Sam often reminded him of her. Why should the boy have been cheated of his mother? Why did she have to die and leave a crippled baby? The big man rubbed his hand over his face. Then he threw his feet over the edge of the bed and stood up.

Sam heard his father moving in the next room. He went to the stove and stirred the fire, then moved the coffee pot to the hottest spot on the stove. Sam knew his father would be hungry and that he wouldn't mind his fixing the fire and moving the coffee pot this once. Jesse felt Sam shouldn't do anything around the house because of his handicap*, so Sam usually didn't. But Sam wanted to now. He found two plates in the cupboard and put them on the table. He and his dad could eat the food that Mrs. Duffey had given them. And they could talk.

"Hey, what's this?" said Jesse Sealth in surprise. "Where did these goodies come from?"

Sam grinned. "Mrs. Duffey gave them to us. They're left from the picnic."

"Oh, so you went on your picnic. Did you have a good time?"

"It was great, Dad. We went to the clearing up on the hill in back of the mill. Guess what we found!" he said remembering Weasel Hole. He told his father about sliding down into the pit and seeing the weasel in the log.

His father nodded his head. "An old gravel pit," he explained. "Did you hurt yourself?"

Sam flushed. He shook his head without saying anything. Then he remembered. "Caleb came—on his horse." He hoped his father would say that Caleb shouldn't have come and spoiled the picnic. But instead he said, "Your brother was just making sure that you were OK."

"I played ball," Sam said after a few minutes.

"*You* played ball? With Peter?"

"No, with Peter's dad. Peter was. . . ." and Sam suddenly remembered the second shadow over the day.

"Peter was what?" his father asked as he cut a slice of cake.

"Oh, he rode Prince—Caleb let him—and he got thrown off. He acted like a baby."

"Did he get hurt?"

"No, he didn't get hurt a bit, but he acted like he did! He'd hardly talk to anybody after that. He didn't even want to play catch. . . . The Duffeys said I can visit them at their ranch. Can I go, Dad?"

Jesse Sealth stood and looked at Sam a long time before he answered. Why were these people being so nice to his crippled son? Other people usually turned away from Sam and had no time for him.

The big man smiled. "We'll see," he said. Then to himself he said, *Duffey—they have the ranch down the river. Jack Duffey is the mechanic I've heard about.*

Jesse Sealth picked up his jacket and lunch pail. "I have to go now. Caleb will be home in an hour. Get yourself off to bed, do you hear?" He put a big hand on Sam's shoulder, then started for the door.

"Dad, do you know about Jesus?" Sam asked.

His father stopped at the door and turned to look at him. In a voice that sounded angry, he said, "No, I don't, Son. . . . Don't eat all that cake. Save some for your brother." He closed the door behind him.

Jesse drove to the mill thinking about Sam's question. He had not heard the name *Jesus* since Maria died. She had often tried to talk to him about Jesus and it had made him angry. He was always too busy to listen or he had found an excuse to do something else. Maria had finally said, "I'm praying for you, Jesse. God will answer my prayers someday."

When Sam asked him about Jesus, he felt the same anger he used to feel before. Where did Sam hear? Was it from the Duffeys?

Jesse sat in his pickup for a few minutes looking at the mill. The sound of the big saws filled the air. The sawdust was piling up into a golden hill. The men were working hard cutting the huge logs into smooth lumber.

A big truck loaded with logs stood in the mill yard. In the morning the fir logs would be cut into lumber. Usually logs were put in the river to keep them from drying out, but not now. The river was too low. The logs would get muddy and the mud would wreck the saws.

The men in the mill office looked up as Jesse Sealth stepped in.

"We've got a problem," one man said.

"Yeah? What is it?" Jesse asked.

"Two of the big trucks broke down. The mechanic at the Trading Center can't get away to work on them, and we sure can't drive them down there."

Jesse had an idea. "Hey, you fellas know Jack Duffey?"

The man who had spoken slapped his leg. "You're right! He's our man. How can we get word to him?"

"I'll have Caleb go." He paused. "Doesn't that beat all? He was here just today. Took Sam on a picnic."

"Took Sam on a picnic?" asked a second man. "Duffey took *Sam* on a picnic?"

"What's wrong with that?" said Jesse hotly.

He left the office in search of Caleb. He found him closing down the saw he had been running. Caleb looked up as he heard his father coming.

"Hi, Dad. Everything OK? Did Sam get back?"

"He's home. He said you went to the picnic."

"I just went to check on him."

Jesse watched Caleb finish his work. He was proud of this boy of his. Tall and muscular, Caleb could outwork any of the others at the mill even though he was only 17. Jesse tried not to compare Caleb and Sam, but it was hard.

Jesse wondered if his older son held any angry or bitter feelings toward Sam. Caleb had been so close to Maria. What had Caleb thought when her life had been traded for a crippled baby? Jesse felt angry again. Where had Maria's "heavenly Father" been when she needed Him? If He was for real, why did she die?

Jesse asked, "Did you meet Jack Duffey?"

Caleb nodded and asked, "Why?"

"He's a good mechanic and we need one."

"The two trucks?" asked Caleb.

"Yeah. Will you take a message to him on Prince?"

"Now?" Caleb asked.

"Go get some sleep first. Check back here in the morning about 8." Jesse turned and walked way.

Caleb walked over to where Prince was tied. The horse was grazing on the grass in the woods. Caleb patted Prince's neck then mounted him and rode off into the night. Other workers were leaving the mill too. Some were in trucks or cars, some on foot, and one or two others on horseback.

Caleb passed homes with lighted windows and thought how it must be to have a mother there waiting. "I have Sam," he said to Prince. "But if I didn't have Sam, maybe I'd have my mother." He said it again to himself. *If I didn't have Sam, maybe I'd have my mother. If Sam were like other kids, it wouldn't be so bad, but— he's so different.*

Caleb went into the room he shared with his brother. Sam was asleep. His blankets had fallen to the floor. Caleb picked them up and spread them over the sleeping boy.

Caleb watched his brother for a minute, then climbed into his own bed. *It won't make any difference to Sam,* Caleb thought, *if I don't take him to the Duffeys. Nothing much matters to Sam, surely not what I do. Sam lives in a world of his own with his scrimshaw.*

Yes, Caleb decided, *I'll go to the Duffeys without him.*

Fire!
5

Peter felt stiff and sore as he climbed out of the jeep. Without saying a word, he carried some of the picnic things into the house. Then he went into his bedroom and closed the door. With his face buried in his pillow, Peter started to cry.

He could hear his parents talking in the kitchen. They had built a fire in the stove and put on the tea kettle. But soon they were talking so softly that Peter couldn't hear them anymore.

After a few minutes, Peter heard his bedroom door open. He clutched the pillow around his ears, hoping his parents would go away. But they didn't.

His father said, "Something's bothering you, Pete. We want to know how we can help."

Silence.

"Peter," his father's voice was a bit demanding, "It will

only get worse unless you tell us about it. Now."

A muffled sound came out of the pillow.

"What?"

"You *laughed* at me!"

"Laughed at you? You mean when you fell off the horse?" his father asked.

"You weren't hurt!" said his mother.

"You laughed at me," repeated Peter.

"We weren't laughing to make fun of you, Peter. We were laughing only because we thought we were laughing *with* you. You did look funny flying through the air. When we saw that you weren't hurt, it seemed alright to laugh," explained his father.

"It hurt when you landed on the ground so hard, didn't it, Pete? And it hurt when you heard us all laughing because you were embarrassed," his mother spoke gently. Peter nodded.

"We didn't mean to embarrass you or to hurt your feelings. Please forgive us!"

"That's right, Son," added his father. "We had no idea we were making your hurt worse. Are we forgiven?"

Peter sat up and brushed his hair out of his eyes and grinned at his mom and dad. They understood him and now he felt better.

"Good!" said his mother in answer to his grin. "Come have some hot chocolate and cookies with us."

Peter got to his feet. He put his hand on the seat of his pants. "Ooh, ow!" Then he laughed as he limped into the kitchen.

Hot chocolate and cookies make any hurt feel better.

Peter finally crawled between the sheets on his bed. He pulled the blankets up to his chin and stared into the dark. He *did* feel better, but there was still that other hurt—Sam laughing at him and his ivory. Peter wished he'd told his mom and dad about that too. Maybe he'd tell them tomorrow.

Quickly he sank deeper and deeper into sleep. He dreamed of horses, ivory, Sam, and Weasel Hole. Other boys and girls were in Weasel Hole too. They danced around in a circle—pointing and laughing. They were laughing at Sam.

Over in the foothills boomed a loud clap of thunder. A flash of lightning lit the sky.

* * *

After Peter finished his morning chores, he wandered out to the pasture. Old Nell was standing under the tree where she always stood. There she was, swishing flies with her tail just as she always did. Peter walked up to her, shrugged his shoulders, and walked away. *What's the use?* he thought.

More than anything else, Peter wanted his own horse. If he had a horse, it would be easier to find rocks for his rock collection. But now he had to hunt rocks on foot. He had already looked in the cave on the hillside and on the banks of the river. *If I had a real horse,* he thought, *I could ride back into the hills and up to the mountains where the old copper and gold mines are. Maybe I could even ride into Golden Canyon.*

"Where's the ivory you were working on, Pete?" Peter

had wandered into the house and watched his mother kneading* bread.

"Oh, I gave that to Sam." Peter pinched off a piece of dough and popped it into his mouth.

"I thought you were going to finish it." Mrs. Duffey divided the dough and put some in each of the three bread pans.

"Oh, it wasn't any good. I couldn't do it. Besides," Peter paused, then blurted out, "Sam laughed at me!"

His mother covered the pans of dough with cloths before she answered. "Sam laughed at you because you couldn't do scrimshaw?"

"Yup," said Peter and picked at the sticky dough still on the kneading board.

Alice sat down. "You were laughed at twice yesterday, weren't you? Both times you felt you were being ridiculed* for something you couldn't help."

"Ridiculed?"

"Yes, ridiculed. You thought Sam was making fun of you and you thought we were making fun of you."

Peter didn't answer.

"Maybe, Pete, the Lord is trying to tell you something."

Peter took a cookie from the cookie jar and walked outside. Past the dog kennels, where the aspen tree leaned out over the fish pool, was a good place to think. Peter slipped off his shoes and socks and let what water there was lap around his ankles.

Peter dropped pebbles into the water and watched the rings they made. Then he remembered his dream from the night before. He saw again the boys and girls all dancing and pointing at Sam. They were all laughing—all but Sam. Pete squeezed his eyes shut tight then opened them. He still saw the circle around Sam.

Peter kept dropping pebbles into the water. He tried to tell himself that he hadn't wanted to laugh at Sam when he first met him. But he *had* wanted to laugh because of Sam's arm and the way he dragged his foot when he walked. Yet Sam could not help those things at all.

Peter looked up at the foothills and the mountains beyond. If he had a horse, he'd be up in those hills and canyons looking for rocks. Suddenly something above the tree tops caught Peter's eye. It looked like a wisp of a cloud forming. *Maybe if a rainstorm comes, the pasture will start growing again and Dad won't have to hay the cattle and sheep till winter,* Peter said to himself.

Peter spotted an unusual rock—then another. While he bent over searching the riverbed, the cloud turned gray. Peter whistled softly to himself. The shifting wind brought him a faint whiff of burning wood.

Peter stood up and drew in a deep breath. There was no mistaking the smell. It was wood smoke coming from the direction of Milltown. Still holding his new rocks, Peter picked his way across the slippery stones, then ran full speed to the house.

"Dad! Mom" he yelled. "I smell smoke! I see it too!"

His mother stepped out on the porch. Her face was flushed from the heat of the cook stove. "Smoke, Pete? It must be from the kitchen stove. I've just built up the fire

and the wind has probably shifted." She turned to go back inside.

"No, Mom. Come and look!" Peter pointed to the northwest.

His mother followed him a few steps from the house and looked in the direction he was pointing. The smoke clouds were turning into mushroom shapes and hiding the sun.

Mrs. Duffey drew in a deep breath as Peter had done, then she whispered, "It *is* a fire!" Turning, she ran toward the field where her husband was mending a broken fence. "Jack! Jack!" she called. "There's a fire—a forest fire! Look! Over there!"

Jack sniffed the air and smelled the smoke. He started for the house.

"It's over near Milltown," he called to his wife. "Lightning must have struck in the hills last night. I'd better drive up there and see if they need any help."

"May I come too, Dad? I won't get in the way!" asked Peter.

"We will probably need all the help we can get," said his father. "Come along. We'll leave as soon as we get a couple of shovels, axes, and rakes. Better take some buckets along too. Mom, will you fix us some lunch to take?"

Quickly they gathered the tools they would need. Peter was almost bursting with excitement. Driving up to Milltown for a picnic was one thing, but knowing there was a fire raging near there was another.

"Jack, *do* be careful," began Peter's mother as she handed them their lunch. "Pete's just a boy and—"

"He'll be *OK*, Alice. I'll keep him right with me. This will be good experience. Don't worry, we'll be back by midnight at the latest."

Trapped!

6

Caleb left his house in plenty of time to be at the mill by 8:00. "I've got to go on a special errand," he told Sam.

Caleb galloped off to the mill. He was talking with his father when he saw something from the corner of his eye. Caleb turned to get a better look. He saw it clearly this time—a cloud of smoke rising from the hills behind the mill.

"Dad! Look! There's smoke!"

Jesse Sealth was beside his son looking. He saw the smoke along with a red flicker on the mountainside. He phoned the lookout tower as fast as he could.

He reported the fire, then listened. "A hundred acres!" he exclaimed. "About three miles northeast of us? He paused then said, "Due southwest? It's heading right for us! Did you call for a chopper*? OK. We'll shut down right away."

The other foremen had come into the office. When Jesse hung up the phone, he said, "A hundred acres are burning and it's headed this way! A chopper and smoke-jumpers* are coming. We'll shut down and head toward the fire. Maybe we can stop it."

The mill's fire siren was screeching before Jesse stopped talking. The saws were all shut off as men answered the siren's call. Their job now was to fight the fire.

Though it was three miles from the mill, the fire moved fast through the dry woods. Trees blazed and the low brush crackled. Like a red monster, the fire killed everything in its path.

Jesse Sealth turned to Caleb. "Get the caterpillar* moving up toward the canyon. We need to start knocking down some of those trees. Tell Mike to take it up."

"What about Jack Duffey?" asked Caleb.

"He'll see the smoke and he'll come. Just go tell Mike to get the cat up there."

Soon the big caterpillar was roaring toward the fire. Mike, the driver, had a wet bandana to cover his nose and mouth. Mike drove the cat within a half-mile of the fire. He knocked down trees and brush in the cat's path. With the big machine, he could knock down 10 trees while a man with a saw chopped down 1. If the fire didn't have the trees and brush to feed on, it would burn itself out.

Other men headed for the fire in jeeps, trucks, and even on foot. They carried shovels, fire rakes, and axes with them. They chopped trees and brush, dug ditches, and raked burning embers away from the dry grass. They had to keep the fire away from the lumber mill. If the mill burned, all of Milltown would burn too.

By now, men and boys from Milltown had joined the mill workers. Mr. Hunter from the Trading Center and the men from the service station had come. Milltown's fire truck was on the scene too. It was ready to send streams of water on the mill and on the ground around it, if the fire got too close.

The first helicopter* from Fairbanks flew overhead just as Jack and Peter Duffey rounded the last curve. Seeing the other jeeps and cars heading behind the mill, Jack knew he must drive on farther. "Hop in," he called to some of the men on foot.

"Dad, there's Sam!"

Sam had heard the siren and had seen and smelled the smoke. By himself, he had started to walk to the mill. People pushed past him. But Sam kept right on walking. He decided not to miss out on the excitement.

"C'mon, Sam," called Peter. "Climb in!"

"Pete, we can't take him!" Jack Duffey scolded.

"Let him come, Dad. He can stay in the jeep where it's safe."

The men who were already in the back of the jeep lifted Sam over the side. "You stay with the jeep, young man," they told him. "The fire line is no place for you."

Flames licked the sky above the trees. For Jack Duffey, it was hard to believe he had come this way for a picnic only the day before. He parked at a safe distance from the fire. "We'll check and see where we're needed," he said.

Caleb tied Prince to a tree close by. From the back of the jeep, the men stepped over Sam and jumped out. Someone put a hard hat on Peter's head. Feeling important, he shouldered a shovel and walked beside his dad, Caleb, and the others.

Sam watched them go. He clung to the side of the jeep with his good hand. He had wanted to fight the fire too, but now he felt useless and left out.

Just then, Sam heard a whinny. He turned and saw Prince pawing the ground. Prince was lonely too—lonely and afraid of the smoke that stung his nostrils and burned his eyes. The horse saw Caleb going ahead without him. He whinnied again. "You're OK, boy," Caleb called.

Peter's eyes watered from the smoke as he hiked the half mile to the fire line. Men coming from the burning woods were black and wet with sweat. Peter stopped and looked up at the helicopter. It flew as low as it could without getting caught in the down-draft*. The down-draft was caused by the hot air from the fire. If the helicopter got caught in it, it might crash.

Peter could see the pilot. There were some other men in the helicopter with him. They were the smoke-jumpers. They had been trained to jump from a plane into smoke to fight a fire. They wore special clothing to protect their bodies. As soon as the pilot was sure of the wind's direction, he hovered at a safe distance and the smoke jumpers parachuted out. They dug more ditches closer to the fire, ditches they hoped the fire would not jump. This way they might stop the fire from moving ahead.

Peter and his dad worked on the fire line, a wide path the fire would not be able to jump. They cut brush and cleared the ground cover.

"Get it all," shouted his father. "If you don't, the fire will."

Peter felt the fire's heat on his face. His back began to ache and his throat felt dry. He heard the cry, "Timmm-ber!" as men cut down the trees the caterpillar did not get.

The hungry fire roared on while trees snapped and fell. The fire was coming closer and closer. The row of men working at the fire line stretched out for half a mile. The fire line was growing, but it wasn't growing fast enough.

"I'm starting a backfire!" Jesse Sealth yelled to the men on the fire line. This second fire would burn toward the big fire and destroy everything in its path. The big fire would have nothing to feed on. There was danger in setting a backfire, if the wind was blowing. Sparks could start new fires.

"If the backfire comes this way and jumps the line," warned Mr. Hunter, "run for it. We'll have to get out of here fast."

Peter heard the caterpillar roaring beyond the line of men. It knocked down a big pine tree, then headed for a clump of aspen trees to widen the fire line. The cat driver pulled quickly across the fire line as the backfire began to burn. A slight breeze picked up the backfire. In seconds, heavy smoke rose almost right in front of them. Then came a burst of flames.

"The fire has crowned!" yelled Jesse. "Pull back! The fire has crowned!"

At that moment, Prince broke from the rope that held him and started up the hill. With sudden strength, Sam climbed from the jeep and chased the horse. He caught hold of the rope, but the scared horse kept running— dragging Sam after him.

Prince stopped to paw the air, giving Sam a chance to get his footing. Just as the boy got a fresh grip on the rope, burning branches crashed down around him and the horse. Sam caught his breath in horror and Prince whinnied more.

The fire jumped to the tops of the trees and over the fire line. Now it would burn even faster than before. Ground cover and the fire line would not be able to stop it. But the backfire might do the job.

Many of the men moved back down the hillside toward the mill. Those who had driven to the fire ran to move their trucks and jeeps. Jack Duffey and Bill Hunter ran and stumbled with Peter and Caleb following close behind them. They would move the jeep to a safer place, then return to fight the fire. Jack was worried about Sam and ran on ahead of the others. But Sam wasn't in the jeep.

As Caleb neared the jeep, he heard Prince whinny. He saw his horse inside a burning thicket, but he didn't see Sam. "Prince!" called Caleb, "Here, boy!" and he gave

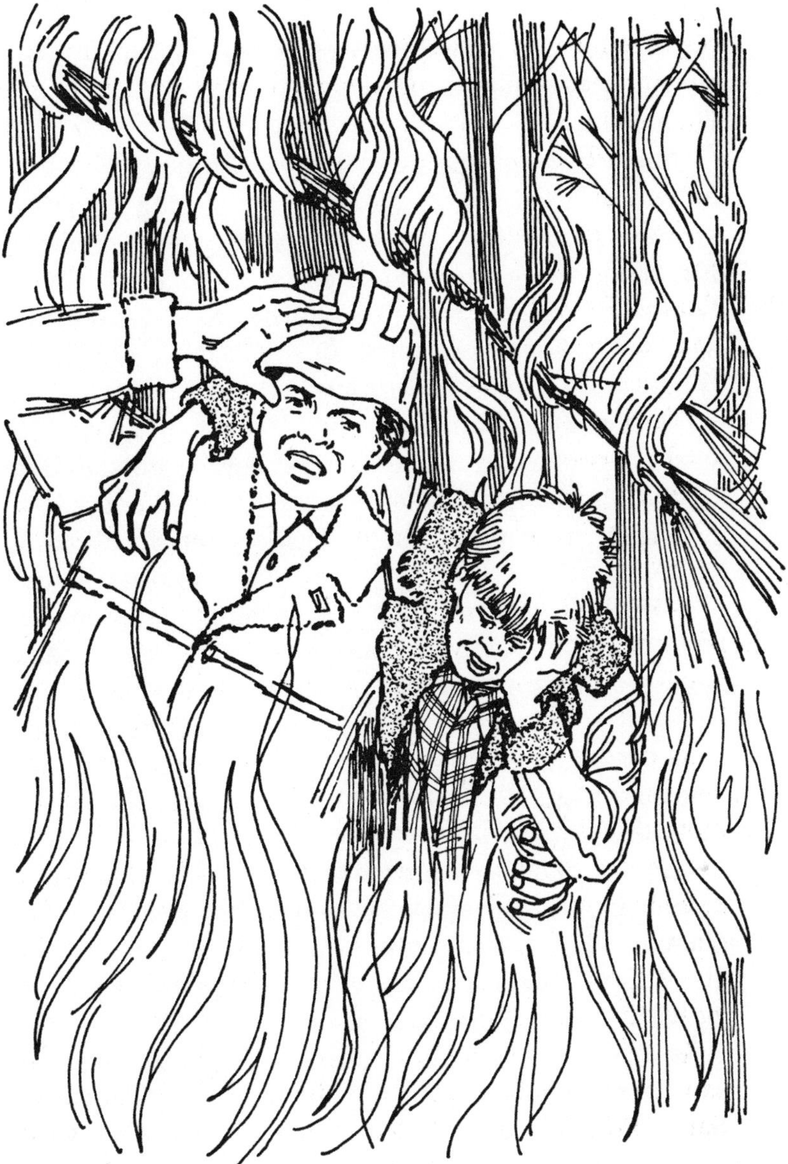

the whistle which Prince always obeyed. With a lunge, the horse tore the rope from Sam's grasp and ran to his master.

The jerk of the rope sent Sam sprawling and knocked off one of his shoes. As he fell, more blazing branches showered around him. Peter saw Sam go down and ran into the burning woods to help him. Quickly he helped Sam stand up. But when they turned to leave, the two saw only the wall of flames.

Peter took a quick look around. The fire itself had not yet met the backfire. There was a space of about 100 yards between the two fires. The boys were standing beside a big flat rock. Peter recognized it as the rock that had been their picnic table. That meant that Weasel Hole and the rocks with the ledge were not far away. Half pushing and half pulling Sam, Peter headed for the hideout. A spray of flying embers hit Peter's hard hat and landed on Sam's bare foot.

To Peter, it seemed that Weasel Hole was miles away. The smoke lifted for a minute and Peter saw the two jagged rocks. He knew Weasel Hole was their only chance.

"C'mon, Sam!" he shouted as he slid down the sandy side of the old gravel pit. He pulled Sam after him and the boy rolled over and over as he had done before. The two crawled across the logs in the bottom of the pit and huddled under the ledge.

Peter closed his eyes. He shivered from the exertion and fear. "Oh, God, save us," he prayed with his eyes shut tight. He opened his eyes and looked at Sam.

"You'd better pray too!" he shouted.

Sam had never prayed before, but he did what Peter told him. "Help, God," he said simply as he looked at the fire in the treetops.

The fire burned on toward the backfire that was coming to meet it. The rocky ledge over the boys felt hot. Weasel Hole filled with smoke and burning embers fell to the bottom, just missing the logs lying there. Two little eyes stared out of the log as the fire ate its way around the edges of the pit and crept across the clearing. As the boys watched wide-eyed with their backs pressed against the rocks, the two fires slowly burned each other out.

Peter had fallen asleep, but now he was wide awake. Sam was still sleeping. His face and arms were smudged with black. One leg of Sam's pants was torn and his bare foot looked red and swollen.

Peter crept out from under the ledge and looked around. Trees that had not fallen under the fire stood black and stripped of their branches. Smoke rose from the black ground. Here and there an ember still glowed. Peter looked at the sky. It must be long after dinnertime.

Where were his dad, Sam's dad, Caleb, and Mr. Hunter? Were they looking for them? Where were the other fire fighters? It was so quiet—too quiet! Was the fire all out? He wondered if he should leave Sam and walk out to where he had left his dad, but he decided not to. The ground was smoking hot. Besides Sam might wake up and be afraid.

Then he heard the big caterpillar. It was coming toward them from where they had run into the woods. Peter stood on the logs on the bottom of the pit. He waved and shouted even before he could see the cat.

Jesse Sealth was driving the caterpillar and Jack Duffey was riding with him. Jack had remembered Weasel Hole. He had felt sure Peter and Sam would go there.

Jack and Jesse saw Peter waving and heard his shout at the same time. "Oh, thank You, Lord," said Jack out loud, "they're safe. Thank You. Peter, you're safe!" He jumped into the pit and took his son in his arms. "Where's Sam?"

He saw Sam as he spoke. The noise of the cat woke Sam and he sat up.

Jesse jumped down beside his son. "You OK, Sam?" Then he saw the boy's burned foot. "Easy does it. We'll get you out of here.

"We'll have to go get a truck or jeep," Jesse said. He turned to Jack. "If we get a barrel of water and wet the ground, will you bring your jeep in?"

"Of course, I will," answered Peter's father. "If the tires get burned, they get burned."

The men looked at their sons. "We're going to leave you, but we'll be back in about half an hour. OK?" Jesse looked at Sam's red, swollen foot again. "You're going to be fine." He took off his shirt and covered his son. "Lie still. We'll hurry back."

Peter watched the cat leave with the two men on it. He shivered again. It wasn't cold, but he didn't want to be left for even half an hour. Sam lay down again and closed his eyes. "Sam?" Peter whispered. "You OK?"

"Yeah, I'm OK," said Sam without opening his eyes. His foot hurt with pain he had never known before. His ears still roared with the sound of the fire that was gone.

Peter sat close to Sam. He wanted to help his friend, but he didn't know how. Before long, he heard the cat coming again. It had a big barrel hooked on and water was spraying from it on to the black ground. The little green jeep followed in the steaming wet path. Pete didn't stand and wave. He sat beside Sam and waited.

Carefully the men laid Sam on some coats in the back of the jeep. Peter climbed in the seat, glad to be near his father once more. Still spraying water, the caterpillar led the way out of the smoking forest.

As they drove out of the fire area, Peter could see flames far down the fire line. Men were still fighting the flames. An amphibian plane* dumped water from the air. At a safe distance, fire fighters who had come from Fairbanks and Anchorage were pitching their tents. They would stay till the vast forest was safe.

Jesse Sealth stopped the cat near the cars and trucks parked beyond the fire. He spoke to Caleb, then climbed into the back of the jeep with Sam. Without a word, Jack drove the jeep out of the woods past the quiet mill and into Milltown. He stopped in front of the Sealth's house. Peter went in with his dad and the two waited with Jesse for the doctor.

When the doctor arrived, he got right down to business. Finally he looked up and smiled, "Sam won't need to be hospitalized," he said. "But he *will* have to be off his feet for a while, two weeks at least."

Jesse ran his hand through his hair. He was relieved that Sam's foot was no worse. He gave the boy a playful punch on the shoulder. "Hear that, Sam? You get to stay in bed and be waited on!" Then he turned and walked to the window.

The doctor knew the question Jesse was asking himself. "Maybe you could get Anna Baker or Mrs. Ticee to come stay with Sam while you and Caleb are at work."

Jesse stood staring out of the window as he shook his head. He said nothing.

"Will you let him come home with us?" Jack stood beside the mill foreman. "Alice can take care of him."

Jesse looked at Jack. "You would take Sam into your home? Your wife may not want this."

"Please say yes, Mr. Sealth." Peter was excited at the idea. "Mom won't care. And she's a good nurse. Really."

Jesse was silent for a few more minutes. He looked at the doctor. "Sounds like a good solution, Jesse. Sam's foot will heal faster if he's well cared for."

"Sam," his father walked over to him. "You're going home with Peter and his dad. Peter's mother will take care of you. As soon as your foot is well you can come home again."

"Go to Peter's house? I can't stay here? W-will you come see me?"

"I'll come when I can, but not every night." Mr. Sealth was not a man to make promises he could not keep. "Caleb and I will both come when we can."

"Boy, is Mom going to be surprised," said Peter as the

jeep drove off. "Three of us instead of only two coming home from the fire!"

It was long past midnight. Though it wasn't completely dark, Jack still turned on the jeep's headlights to help him see his way through the woods.

Jesse Sealth stood on his porch, watching the jeep disappear. *What am I doing,* he wondered, *letting Sam go off with the Duffeys? Will they really take good care of him even though he's handicapped?* He felt lonesome for Sam already.

"Dad," Sam's voice echoed in his heart, "do you know Jesus?"

At Home with the Duffeys

7

The early morning sun woke Alice. She lay still, feeling she had had a bad dream—then she remembered. She had waited hours for her husband and her son to come home from the fire. She had watched the smoke grow thicker and thicker. She had even seen some flashes of flames when the fire had crowned.

Alice had tried to wait up for Jack and Peter, but she had dozed off in a chair. The sound of the jeep had startled her. "Alice!" Jack had called as he stumbled onto the porch with Sam in his arms. Half asleep, Peter had wandered in behind his father.

"Thank God, you're home," Alice had said. "Sam?"

"His foot's burned, Hon," Jack had explained simply. "Peter told Sam's dad you're a good nurse."

Jack had laid Sam on the extra bed in Peter's room. Then he turned to his own son. "He's been a real hero,

Mom. But right now he's a tired one. Into bed with you." Almost before his dad finished speaking, Peter was asleep.

Now as Alice lay in bed, she listened for sounds from the next room. Slipping into her robe, she quietly went into Peter's room. Her son lay with his head half off the bed. One foot peeked out from under the blankets that were pulled up around his shoulders. Soot and dirt were still on his face. Alice smoothed his hair and kissed him lightly on the cheek. Peter moved onto his pillow and drew his foot back under the covers.

Alice turned to Sam, who was staring at her. He had seen her come into the room. He had watched as she stooped and kissed Peter.

"Hi, Sam," whispered Alice gently. Aware of the sadness in his eyes, she smoothed his hair as she had Peter's and kissed Sam on the cheek. "How does your foot feel?"

Sam didn't know what to say. Alice smiled and touched his hair again. "It will be well in no time. The doctor sent some medicine to put on it and some pills for you to take if it hurts too much. You be sure and let me know, won't you, when it hurts real bad. I'm going to start the fire now and get us some breakfast. If Pete and his dad wake up, they can have some too."

Alice disappeared into the kitchen. Sam heard her shake the ashes in the stove and lay the new fire. He heard the crackling of the kindling and the water running into the tea kettle. The boy closed his eyes. Was all of this real or had he died in the fire and gone to heaven?

That was *his* mother who had kissed him and *his* mother who was making breakfast sounds in the kitchen. He lay quietly.

"Psst, Sam. You awake?" Heaven faded as Sam opened his eyes and saw Peter looking at him. Pain shot through his foot.

Peter's dad stood in the doorway. "Morning, fellas," he said cheerfully. "It's time to get this day started. Pete, go scrub off that dirt. Sam, I think I can scrub you without hurting that foot. Mom's got breakfast almost ready, so we'll wait till after we've eaten."

"Are you going to Milltown today, Dad, to fight the fire?" asked Peter.

Jack shook his head. "There are enough professional fire fighters there now. Besides it's almost under control."

* * *

"Can I get you some more, Sam?" Alice asked from the kitchen. Sam, propped up on pillows in bed, had never eaten such feathery-light pancakes.

"No, thank you, ma'am," he said politely. He felt he could eat them forever, but he had had eight and he was sure he should say no.

"Time for devotions," called Peter from the kitchen. "Let's all sit on Sam's bed."

"We'll sit on *your* bed," his mother said with a laugh.

"Let's read from Psalm 91 this morning," Jack Duffey suggested. Peter found the place in his Bible and shared it with Sam. Peter's father read out loud.

"He will cover you with His pinions, and under His wings you may seek refuge; His faithfulness is a shield and bulwark. You will not be afraid of the terror by night, or of the arrow that flies by day. . . . For He will give His angels charge concerning you, to guard you in all your ways. They will bear you up in their hands, lest you strike your foot against a stone."

"Pete, do those verses have any special meaning for you?" his father asked.

"Oh yes, Dad." Peter remembered the horror and the heat of the fire. "My guardian angel was really with me, wasn't he?" The boy's eyes grew wide with wonder. "He led us to safety, he really did!"

Sam could keep quiet no longer. "What's a guardian angel?"

"God has assigned an angel to everyone of His children, Sam," explained Pete's father, "to take care of them. Pete is a child of God. His angel led you two to safety and took care of you. There's no doubt about it."

"We—we could've died in the fire, couldn't we, Dad?" asked Peter.

"Very easily," answered his father. "Either one or both of you could easily have died. Sometimes God does take children home to be with Him, but yesterday He spared you."

"Dad, yesterday I said, 'God help us,' and—and He did!" Peter's eyes were shining with the thrill of answered prayer.

"Peter," his mother spoke slowly, "God spared you for a reason."

"It's because I'm His child."

"I know, Pete. But God wants to show you what He wants you to do—not just what *you* want. Understand? And Sam, too. I'm sure God has a plan for Sam's life."

"Peter," said his father, "why don't you pray first this morning?"

"OK," Peter put his face in his hands. "Dear God," he took a deep breath, "Thank You, God, for saving me and Sam yesterday. It was awful hot and we were both scared, but You knew all about it and saved us. Now You can do whatever You want with me. Please make Sam's foot well, but not too fast 'cause, it's fun having him here."

Jack added to Peter's prayer. "Father, thank You for sparing these boys. Grant us wisdom in guiding and training Peter. We know you have a special plan for his life—and for Sam's life too. Touch Sam's heart and the hearts of his father and brother so they may be Your children. Be with those who are still on the fire line. In Jesus' name. Amen."

"Amen," whispered Alice. Peter glanced at his mother, then looked away. It embarrassed him when there were tears on her cheeks.

"Chores, Pete." Jack Duffey stood up. He turned to Sam. "You're my first chore this morning, young man. Into the tub with you! Pete, start the water. Mom, get the towels—and away we go!" Before he could protest, Sam was lifted in two strong arms with his burned foot held high.

* * *

Three days had passed since the fire. Sam's burned foot hurt and the medicine Mrs. Duffey gave him made him sleepy.

When he wasn't napping, Sam watched Peter closely. He kept thinking of what Pete's dad had said, that Pete was a child of God. If Pete were a child of God, he must be different than what he, Sam, was. Sam wanted to know what the difference was.

He saw that Peter did the chores his dad told him to do. But Sam did what his father asked him to do too—only his father didn't ask him to do much because he was handicapped. Peter did what his mother asked him to do, but Sam knew that if his mother were alive, he would do all that she asked and more.

Sam thought about the fire. Peter didn't have to go into the woods to help him. Peter might have gotten burned even worse than he himself had. Peter could even have died in the fire. *That must be it,* thought Sam. *Peter wasn't afraid to go into the fire to help me even when he might have died. That must be it, Peter was a child of God because he wasn't afraid to die for somebody else.*

Then Sam wondered if what he had done at the fire was good enough to make him a child of God. He wanted very much to be one. But maybe God didn't care about horses.

While Alice Duffey cooked dinner, Peter set up a game of checkers for Sam and himself to play.

"Sam, do you want red or black?"

"I don't care. I. . . ."

"Say one or the other. Say 'red' or 'black.' "

"OK. Black." Then after a moment Sam said, "Pete, can I ask you something?"

"Huh? You move first. You're company. What do you want, Sam? Your foot hurt worse?" Peter looked anxiously at his friend.

Sam shook his head and moved a black checker. "What would've happened if we'd died in the fire?"

"We'd have been burned up I guess." Peter moved a red checker.

"I mean—what about God? What would He do with us, if we'd died?" He jumped Peter's red checker with his black one.

"We'd go be with Him in heaven. At least I would."

"What about me? Would I go too?"

"No, not unless you're His child too. Everybody who's not God's child goes to hell." He jumped a black checker with his red one.

"Boy, oh boy," Peter went on. He took his hand from the checkerboard. "Imagine how hot hell is. That forest fire—hell's a lot hotter than that—and *that* was hot!"

"My mom's in heaven," said Sam.

"How do you know?"

"Dad told me."

"Just cause a person's dead . . ." began Peter, then he stopped. "That's great," he said instead.

"Why did you go into the woods after me?" asked Sam after a few moments.

Peter studied the checkerboard for his next move. "Mmm, I guess 'cause I didn't want you to die."

"You were willing to die for me," said Sam.

"Something like that," answered Peter. "Yeah, I guess so."

"Is that what makes you a child of God?"

"Because I went into the woods after you? Nope. That doesn't make me God's child. But God made me strong so I could do it. Your move."

"What else does a child of God do?"

"Oh, they *don't* do a lot of things. They don't lie, for one thing. And they don't hate and they don't envy or get mad. And they don't—Mom, what's that word that begins with *l*? It means to want money and things and stuff."

"Do you mean lust?" came the answer from the kitchen.

"That's it. They don't lust. Mom, where's Dad going?"

"No place. Why?"

"I hear the jeep."

"Dad's in the garden. Oh, I hear it too. It's a pickup. . . . Sam, your dad and another man are here."

As Sam turned to look, the checkerboard tipped and red and black checkers rolled to the floor. He heard his father's voice in the kitchen and the doctor's laugh. "We're looking for a boy called Sam," said his father. "Can you tell us where to find him?"

"In here, I think," joked Alice as she led the men to where the boys were.

"Well, young fella, how's that foot?" asked the doctor

after Sam's dad had greeted the boy. Gently the doctor removed the bandage and examined the burn. "It's doing great, just great. You'll be walking on it before you know it."

"Can't he hop now?" asked Peter.

"Hop?" asked the doctor.

"Hop on one foot—then he could go outside."

"I-I can't hop!" cried Sam.

"How about crutches?" Peter kept trying. "Don't you have some crutches he could use?"

"I can't use crutches either," Sam said, then he turned his face away from Peter.

Peter saw his friend's twisted arm lying on top of the covers. "I'm sorry, Sam," he said.

"We sure miss you at home," said Jesse in a husky voice.

"How's Caleb and how's Prince?" asked Sam.

"Fine, real fine. Prince has a blister on his rump, but otherwise he's OK. Caleb's fine. He took some time off from work to rest up from the fire, but he went back to the mill today."

"And Charger? How's he?"

"He misses you too. Say," Jesse snapped his fingers, "that gives me an idea!"

"What is it, Dad?"

"Never mind for now. We'll see."

"You men will stay and have dinner with us, won't you?" asked Alice. "It's nearly ready."

Over steak and bowls full of creamed new potatoes and garden fresh beans, the four grown-ups talked about the fire and the wonder of having the boys safe.

"It took a lot of courage for what they both did," said the doctor. "Courage to risk going after a horse and courage to risk going after another boy. It isn't everybody who would have that kind of courage."

"God was with them," Alice was saying softly. "His ways are always perfect. He takes care of His own."

Jesse looked up. "If there is a God, and His ways are perfect, why did he let Sam be born crippled?" he asked. It had hurt him to hear his son say "I can't hop" and "I can't use crutches."

There was silence around the table. Sam listened from the bedroom. Hadn't he asked himself the same things his father was asking?

The doctor broke the silence. "There is a God, Jesse. Every time I see a baby born I know there's a God. You see His work yourself in every tree and in every mountain."

"God created us." Jack Duffey laid down his fork as he spoke. "He made us the way He wants us. There's a Bible verse that speaks of God being like a potter who shapes His clay any way He wants. But what He makes out of that clay can be used for something beautiful."

"It's not Sam's legs or arms that really matter," said Alice. "It's what's in his heart—that's the real boy. Maybe his body is different, but Sam is a person with feelings just like his brother or Peter or any other boy. And he has every right to be loved and treated like anyone else."

"Have all of the fire fighters gone home?" asked Jack, changing the subject.

"They're still fighting a brush fire on the east side of Trapper's Canyon, but mostly it's under control. Over 200 acres were destroyed."

"Do you want anything more, Sam?" asked Alice rising to wait on the boy. "Pete will bring you a piece of pie, if you're ready. Better eat a big piece 'cause your dad is taking the rest home for Caleb." She smiled at Jesse.

After dinner Jesse talked to Sam. "Oh here, I brought you this. It was on the kitchen table." He drew Sam's piece of ivory from his pocket. "I thought you might like to work on it."

Sam grinned at his dad. "What's the idea you had, Dad?" he asked.

"Never you mind," his dad answered. "I said we'd see about it later. One more thing, then we must go." Jesse turned to Jack. "We need a mechanic at the mill and I hear you're tops. How about it?"

Jack glanced at Alice. "I'd be interested in talking about it. You know I've got the farm work and. . . .

"Part-time maintenance work during the summer and general overhaul on equipment when we're shut down during the winter," Jesse assured him. "We have two rigs that need some work now. Think about it." Turning to Alice he said, "I can't say how much your taking care of Sam means to me."

"We enjoy him," said Alice. "He's a good patient and no trouble."

"Take care, Son, and do as you're told." Jesse playfully punched Sam's shoulder. "I won't be able to see you for a couple of days."

The men walked to the door. "About that idea I have," Jesse said to Jack as his voice trailed off into the night air.

Sam Learns a Lesson

8

I'm going to teach Sam how to wash dishes! thought Alice Duffey as she cleared the breakfast table. *Let's see now. I'll put the high stool in front of the sink and open the cupboard doors underneath. This box should be high enough to rest his foot on. There.*

"Sam," she said out loud, "I want you to wash the dishes." She stood looking down at the surprised boy.

"I—I can't," stammered Sam.

"Why do you say you can't?" demanded Alice.

"Because—well, I can't. I'm—I'm handicapped."

"No, I didn't know," said Alice, pretending to be surprised. "You have a burned foot that is 24-hours better than it was this time yesterday. Sam, don't hide behind your handicap. God wants you to grow around it and because of it—not shrink behind it. Now come on. You are going to wash dishes!"

"I can't hold the dishes." Sam felt a new kind of fear. What if he tried and failed?

"Oh, yes you can," said Alice. "You can hold your ivory when you do scrimshaw. A dish is no heavier than a small piece of ivory—so you can hold one and wash it. Now come!"

"How am I going to get out there?"

"Oh!" For a minute Alice felt baffled. "I have it!" she said and disappeared into the bedroom. She got the old desk chair on castors* and pushed it to the couch. "Here, get on this."

Sam was afraid to try. "If you can go into a forest fire, you can try this," encouraged Alice.

With Alice's help, Sam moved slowly onto the chair. His trip to the kitchen was quick. But getting him onto the stool nearly ended in failure, for the chair kept rolling away. Finally Sam was perched on the stool. He put his hands in the soapy dish water. "Wash them clean, rinse them, and put them in the drainer. I'll be in the bedroom." Alice smiled happily to herself.

Sam let the hot water wash over his hands. He watched the rainbow colored bubbles burst on his finger. Carefully he took a saucer with his right hand, placed it in his left hand, then washed both sides. Saucer by saucer, cup by cup, plate by plate. Alice came from the bedroom. "You're doing fine," she said as she looked over the drainer full of dishes. "You *can* wash dishes, Sam. You're doing a great job."

Sam beamed. "Can I dry them too?"

"Well, I'm sure you can and you may. Be my guest.

Tomorrow Pete and his dad will be picking beans. You can help me get them ready to can. My, I'm glad you're here to help me!"

Sam smiled as he studied his water-wrinkled hands. Helping and knowing he was being useful made him feel different on the inside. He couldn't help smiling.

* * *

"Come on, Pete, let's go take a look at the sheep." Peter's dad climbed into the jeep. "We'd better throw some hay out for them since the pasture is so dry."

They made their way across the pasture and over a dry creek bed. The sheep were grazing on the far side under the aspen trees. Peter looked over the open country. Shaded by trees, the opening to Golden Canyon was almost hidden. As if reading his son's thoughts, Jack said, "Someday we'll explore that canyon together. Don't ever go there alone—there are too many grizzly bears."

"Count the sheep, will you?" asked his father after they had driven a few more minutes. "There were 30 ewes and 27 lambs last count. Plus the 2 rams."

The jeep drove slowly around the edge of the pasture so it wouldn't frighten the gentle animals. Their winter wool had been cut off in the early summer and they still looked sleek and slim. The new wool was just starting to grow in. Peter moved to the back of the jeep. He tossed out the hay at the same time that he counted the sheep.

"Same count, Dad," he said when the jeep had circled the entire pasture. "Thirty ewes and 27 lambs. Dad, could I sell my lambs?"

"Sell your lambs? Why?"

"To buy a horse."

"No, Pete. The money from next year's wool from those lambs is for your schooling—just like this year's was."

"But you're going to be a mechanic for the mill," said Peter.

"Pete, if I am a mechanic for the mill whatever money comes in will be needed for other things. Mother needs a new washing machine. I need a new tractor. Right now, a horse is a luxury."

"What if I save money to buy one and the hay to feed him? Not my sheep money," he hurried to add.

"When you do that," said his father, "we'll talk about it." He drove on silently for a few minutes then asked, "How do you plan to earn the money?"

"I don't know yet." Peter looked at the foothills in back of the pasture. If he could only get up there, maybe he could find some special rocks. But he needed a horse to get there and Old Nell would never make it. Sam sold scrimshaw at the Trading Center, maybe he could sell some rocks.

"Someone's coming," said Peter as the jeep stopped by the barn. The dogs by the river had started barking. "Look over there—on horseback."

Caleb waved as he rode up to Peter and Jack Duffey. Behind him on a lead rope was Charger, Sam's black and white horse.

"Hi, Caleb. I've been expecting you," said Jack. "Your dad said you might bring Sam's horse today. How are you, Prince?" Jack began petting the soft velvet nose that bobbed up and down as Prince snorted a greeting.

"He's great," said Caleb as he swung to the ground.

Peter was patting Charger. "How's Sam going to ride his horse with his burned foot?"

"This was Sam's dad's idea. Sam can ride for a few minutes at a time even if his foot is burned. This way he can get out of the house and have something to do. Besides Charger is something of his own from home."

"Oh," said Peter. It didn't seem fair that Sam had this beautiful horse when he couldn't have one.

"Maybe you can learn to ride Charger too," said Caleb. "Maybe your dad will help you."

"Sure," said Peter feeling sorry for himself, "maybe he will!"

Peter's father gave him a sharp look. "Get some water for the horses. We're going inside."

Sam looked up with a grin as Caleb came in the door.

"Hi, Sam," said the older boy. "I came to see how you're doing. Have you been causing any trouble?"

"Nope, I'm fine," answered Sam. "How's Prince?"

Caleb jerked his thumb towards the door. "He's out there. Come see for yourself." He picked up his brother and carried him to the porch.

"Charger!" Sam cried when he saw his own horse. "You brought Charger! Oh, now I know," he looked at Caleb slyly, "that was Dad's big idea."

"You're right. Want to go for a ride?"

"Oh boy, can I?"

Peter stepped into the shadow of the barn as Caleb put

Sam on Charger, then mounted Prince. "Just for a few minutes," warned Alice from the porch. "His foot can't be down for long."

The two horses walked off together toward the pasture. "Sam, why did you do it?"

"Why did I do what?"

"Why did you save Prince when you might've been killed?"

"Prince is part of you and I just wanted to save him," answered Sam. "I guess I wanted to show you I could do something."

"You were willing to maybe die so you could show me you could do something?" Caleb was quiet while he thought about it.

"Peter said something about how good it is to lay down your life for your friend. Only you're my brother."

"Where did Peter hear that?"

"He reads it in the Bible He said Jesus said it."

"Before you were born," said Caleb. "I remember mother talking about Jesus. She read the Bible a lot. She read it to me and sang songs about Jesus."

"Our mother did that? Then she's in heaven, she really is!"

"Guess so!"

They rode to the apple tree, down to the dog kennels, then back to the barn. Sam was glad to stop when they got back to the barn. His foot was hurting again and he was tired.

"Your turn, Peter," said Caleb as he lifted Sam off.

Peter shook his head and stayed by the barn. He

remembered how they had laughed when he fell off Prince. Besides, Charger was Sam's horse and Peter wanted a horse of his own.

Jack Duffey spoke in a low voice. "I want you to get on that horse. Caleb will hold the reins and lead him, won't you, Caleb?"

"Sure, he won't buck you, Pete. C'mon."

Peter found the stirrups with his toes and held tightly to the saddle horn. Once around the barn and he began to feel the rhythm of the horse. "Hey, you're doing great," said Caleb. "Here, take the reins. Don't be scared. I'll still hold the bridle."

Peter rode around the barn twice more, then over to the pasture fence and back to the barn. He felt proud, like a king. Someday—someday he would have his own horse.

"You can ride OK," said Caleb as Peter slid off. "All you need is practice."

Peter was still feeling glad when he set up the checkers for his evening game with Sam. He forgot about being jealous. He could ride a horse, hadn't Caleb said so? And nobody, but nobody had laughed! Besides, he had a plan—a secret plan he did not dare share with anyone.

* * *

The next day Peter studied every move as his father saddled Charger for Sam. His dad pulled the cinch* tight and fastened it, then slipped the bridle over the horse's head. Peter stood by without a word as Sam went for a short ride. Then he asked, "May I please try again, Dad?"

He mounted by himself while his dad held the reins. He rode toward the dog kennels. Then he went down to the apple tree, around the barn, and to the chicken house pulling on the reins and speaking softly to the horse. He stopped beside Old Nell and let the two horses stand together for a few minutes. On his third time around, his father stopped him.

"Come on, Pete. There's work to do. Put Charger over with Old Nell."

Peter worked beside his dad picking the beans for canning. A cloud passed over the sun and more were on the horizon. "I think we might get some rain after all of these weeks," said his dad.

Peter stood up and looked down the long rows of the garden. The corn stalks were tall and their tassels waved in the breeze. Peter bent again to his task, his mind too busy with his secret plan to talk to his father.

Inside the house, Alice had Sam sitting at the kitchen table. His leg was stretched out on another chair. She placed a cutting board and knife beside him. "You hold the beans like this." She held several beans together tight against the board. "And do this." She cut off the ends. "Then cut them in half and drop them in the pan."

"I'm not sure I. . . ." began Sam.

"Sam," Alice was shaking her knife at him, "I don't want to hear that again! Say 'I'll try.' " She turned and worked at the sink in silence for a few minutes.

"You're doing it just right." She stopped to watch her

pupil. "Make that left hand hold the beans tight. You know, Sam, you can have the power to do anything that's right and good that comes your way to do. God will give you the power to do what He asks you to do." She turned back to the sink.

"My mother's in heaven," said Sam as he worked on his beans.

"Yes, I know." Sam had said this before.

"Caleb told me," he said.

"Caleb told you your mother's in heaven? Your dad has told you too, hasn't he? How does Caleb know?"

"When he was little, she talked to him about Jesus."

"That's good to know," said Alice softly.

"I wonder what all she did," Sam said as he looked out of the window at the cloudy sky.

"I'm sure she did many good and lovely things," said Alice. She did not know what Sam was thinking.

Sam sighed. "I want to go to heaven where my mom is, and I want to be able to do things without being afraid."

"You can, Sam. You can be where she is. Do you—" Alice Duffey started.

At that moment Peter opened the screen door. "Here's another basket full, Mom. Do you want some cucumbers? Dad wants to know. He says you should come out and see the size of some of them."

Alice left Sam sitting at the table while she went to the garden. Sam looked at the pile of beans on the table and at the basket Peter had just brought in. Maybe saving Prince wasn't enough. Sam said to himself, *Mrs. Duffey did say that I can be where my mother is. So maybe if I work really hard and try to do good things—maybe I will get to heaven too. Mrs. Duffey would like it, if I fix all of these. There sure are a lot of them!* Sam chopped the beans as fast as he could.

The day's work was finally over. In the kitchen 32 quarts of beans stood on the cupboard. Cucumbers floated in a crock of brine waiting to be made into pickles. Sam was stretched on the couch working on his scrimshaw.

Peter watched from a safe distance, hoping Sam wouldn't ask him to try. The horseback riding had worked out fine, but doing scrimshaw wouldn't, he knew.

"Are you going to take that to the Trading Center?"

"Maybe. Mr. Hunter might like it."

"Why don't you show Sam some of your rocks, Pete," suggested his dad.

"Oh, OK. I have some work to do on them anyway." Peter placed a box of them on the table and chose some to show Sam.

"Hey, these are neat," admired Sam. "What's this one?"

"It's an agate. This is a piece of quartz, this blue one is turquoise, and this one is jade."

"How come they're so bright and shiny?"

"I tumble them."

"Tumble them?"

"Sure. I put them in a tumbler* and it cleans and polishes them while it tumbles them. Tomorrow I'll show you." Peter felt warmed by Sam's interest.

"You could make jewelry—necklaces and stuff for ladies."

"S'pose I could." Peter took a small rock and an index card. He decided to share part of his secret plan. "But I thought I could glue a rock on a card, with the name of the rock and where it was found printed on the card."

Jack looked up from the book he was reading and listened. He and Alice looked at each other. "Do you plan to sell them at the Trading Center?" he asked his son.

"They're probably no good." Peter began to put his rocks away. He was half sorry he had shared even that much of his plan.

"I think it's an excellent idea, Peter," his mother spoke quickly. "Tourists would buy those, I'm sure."

Peter gave his mother a grateful look. "I've got to find some more small ones—most of these are too big."

"We can cut the big ones, you know," his father said.

"Could we?" Peter hadn't thought of that. "But I still need some smaller ones."

Alice laid her sewing down and walked over to Sam. He folded his hand over the ivory he was working on. Alice pretended not to notice.

"Come look at his foot, Jack. Don't you think he can start using it?"

"Looks good to me," agreed her husband. "The doctor said two weeks and it's been just about that. It sure has healed nicely. How about it, Sam? How does it feel?"

"Pretty good," said Sam. If his foot was well, there was no need for him to stay at the Duffeys' any longer. But he wasn't sure he was ready to go home yet.

"Try standing on it," said Jack.

Peter watched as Sam tested his foot. *If Sam's foot is well, he will be going home soon and so will Charger,* Peter thought. *If I'm going to carry out my secret plan, I'd better do it soon.*

Peter put his rocks back in the box and stretched with a wide, noisy yawn. "Guess I'll be going to bed." He yawned again.

"To bed? You haven't had your game of checkers yet!" His mother looked surprised.

"I'm tired. Picked too many beans I guess. You play checkers with Sam, Mom. 'Night,"

Peter closed the bedroom door quietly. He crawled into bed with his clothes on. "It'll save time in the morning," he reasoned.

He shut his eyes tight. "Four o'clock, four o'clock," he repeated over and over. "I want to wake up at four o'clock." He didn't dare set his alarm clock. Once before, he had told himself when to wake up and it had worked. "Four o'clock, four o'clock," he whispered into his pillow.

Golden Canyon

9

When he awoke, Peter could see the sky was cloudy. A soft rain had started to fall. He stared at the sky for a while, then he remembered why he was awake. He sat up slowly and looked at Sam. The boy was facing toward Peter, but seemed deep in sleep.

Peter lifted his blankets and crawled out. Picking up his socks and boots, he turned the door knob gently. He tiptoed into the kitchen just as the clock on the wall struck 4. He stood there in the kitchen, half expecting a sleepy voice to call his name. There was no sound except the ticking of the clock.

Sam raised up on one elbow and stared at the door as Peter pulled it shut. He had heard Peter step out of bed. He had watched as he picked up his boots. Sam knew it was very early and sensed that there was something very secret about what Peter was doing.

Sam lay and listened for a few minutes. Maybe Peter would come back to bed. The clock chimed four times. Sam heard Peter open the back door and close it. He turned over and pulled the blankets up around his shoulders. Soon he was sound asleep again.

Peter pulled on his socks and boots while he stood on the porch. He took his rain jacket off the hook and then walked to the barn. The rain felt cool and damp on his face, the latch of the barn door was wet in his hand.

Old Nell whinnied as Peter came close. Charger answered. "Shhh," warned Peter. "Good Nell, nice ol' girl." He put out a can of oats to quiet her.

"Good Charger, good boy." He gave Charger some oats, then picked up the saddle blanket and tossed it over the horse's back. It took two tries to get the saddle on. Charger munched on the oats while Peter pulled the cinch belt tight. The bridle slipped over the horse's head and Charger took the bit as though he knew he was a part of Peter's plan.

Throwing another handful of oats to Old Nell, Peter picked up an empty grain sack and led Charger out of the barn—forgetting to latch the door behind him. He stepped around the garden, pulled several carrots, then walked the horse past the dog kennels. He whispered to the dogs to keep them quiet.

Not until he was across the river and out of sight of the house did Peter mount Charger. It took three tries to get into the saddle. The boy glanced at the sky. It was impossible to tell the sun's position. Two hours was all the time he dared take, Peter decided. If he were back home by 6 o'clock when his dad got up, no one would know he had gone any farther than the dog kennels. They might not even know he had gone at all! Peter knew he would have to make his two hours count.

Water ran off his rain jacket and dripped from his hat. The leaves and branches of trees hit his face as Charger kept on the trail that led back into the foothills. Wild berry bushes, scrub birch, and pine grew thick along the trail. It wasn't easy to see where the canyon began since the opening was so well hidden. Peter hadn't really planned to go into Golden Canyon. He hadn't meant to disobey his father. He just wanted to find more rocks to sell.

On and on Charger went. The rain had stopped now and a heavy mist had settled over the hillside. Peter could smell the pine needles and blueberries. He pulled a carrot from his pocket and wiped it on his pants. With it in his mouth, he spoke to Charger, "Come on boy, just a bit farther."

The canyon walls were getting steep. Peter looked at the boulders and trees high above him. A moose walked through the trees ahead of him. Suddenly he saw what he wanted. Along the edge of the canyon was a dry stream bed filled with rocks. On the side of the canyon wall were the remains of an old wooden sluice*.

Peter remembered the stories of how miners stood by the sluice for hours, letting water from the stream wash over the coarse sand they had shoveled into the box. Across the bottom of the sluice the miners had nailed bars of wood. Onto these they poured precious quicksilver or mercury. Then as the water from the stream washed away the sand and gravel, the gold would be caught and held by the heavier quicksilver. With the sand all gone, the miners would remove the precious yellow metal. They kept doing this until they had enough to sell. Sometimes the gold was as fine as sand. Other times there would be bigger nuggets.

Charger lowered his head to graze. Peter's imagination was so strong he thought for a moment that a gnarled willow tree was an old miner hard at work. He squeezed his eyes shut to make what he imagined disappear. Around him were rocks of all shapes, sizes, and colors. He had to work fast. He slid off Charger and chose the most colorful rocks. He picked up one and then another. He dropped them into the grain sack he had brought along.

He moved closer and closer to the old sluice. He wondered what it had been like to be a miner. He took hold of the side. But the old, rotten board fell off in his hand. Carefully he stood on a large stone so he could see inside. A few of the bars (an old trapper had called them riffles) were still nailed in place. Peter pulled at one riffle. The rotten wood gave way here too. Under the riffle was a small line of sand that had been there for as long as the miner had been gone. Peter ran his finger through the sand. A small golden stone glistened in the light.

"Wow! I wonder if there's any more."

Peter began tearing off riffles. He found three more smaller stones. Next he hunted along the edges of the

sluice. He put every golden pebble he could find into his shirt pocket.

The blueberry bushes grew thick around the old sluice and berries hung heavy on them. Every morning, a mother grizzly bear and her cubs slowly walked down the side of the canyon, eating the juicy berries for their breakfast. They had always had this side of the canyon to themselves. But not this morning. Mother Grizzly poked her nose into a very large blueberry bush and saw Charger's nose. She growled deep in her throat and stood on her hind legs.

Peter was so interested in the gold that he paid no attention to the crackling of the twigs. Not until he heard Charger whinny did he look up. Charger, standing on his hind legs was hitting at something with his fore legs. The mother grizzly on her hind legs slapped at the horse. A line of red showed on Charger's shank as he turned and ran full speed down the trail.

Peter was afraid to call Charger—the bear was too close. He froze tight against the sluice and held his breath. He watched the bear. Satisfied she had chased away her enemy, she headed off into the woods. Two cubs followed at her heels.

Peter let his breath out slowly. His desire for rocks was gone. All he wanted now was to be safe at home. But he was miles away from the ranch. Golden Canyon looked so far away when he saw it from the pasture and now he was standing in the middle of it! Maybe, just maybe Charger had stopped part way down the trail to graze and was waiting for him.

The mist had cleared by now and the sun was hot. Steam rose from the wet bushes and mossy ground. Peter looked down as he stepped off the rock he'd been standing on. He saw something that looked like an old leather bag. Stooping to look at it, he saw that it was an old pouch that a miner would have used to carry his gold. The pouch was not empty. Spilling out of it were several gold nuggets and inside were more. Peter started to pick it up. But like the sluice, it was old and rotten— and ripped. He took a handkerchief out of his pocket and carefully wrapped the pouch, gold and all, in it and tucked it into his pocket. Then grasping a big stick, he began to pick his way carefully so as not to make any noise that might attract the bear. Slowly, very slowly, he worked his way through the underbrush while looking back over his shoulder.

Charger stopped for nothing. The wound on his shank felt like a hot iron. When he was out of the canyon, he stopped and sniffed the air. Not sure which way to go, he gave a whinny and in the distance he heard a faint answer. Old Nell, still in the barn, was calling to her friend to come home.

Alice was standing at the kitchen sink. The clock had struck 7:30. She was filling the tea kettle when she saw Charger trotting by.

"Jack, look!" Her husband came and stood beside her.

"Well, my word." Jack turned to the boys' room and opened the door. Sam looked up at him. "Where's Peter?" demanded Jack.

Sam shook his head on his pillow. "I don't know."

*   *   *

Peter knew Charger had gone on ahead of him. He knew too that his father would see the horse, saddle and all, and would be angry with him for having gone into Golden Canyon alone when he had told him not to.

Peter stopped to pick some blueberries. *Why should I tell Dad that I've been in the canyon? I've just been out for an early morning ride on Charger, that's all.* His dad would guess it was from the barn to the dog kennels and up to the apple tree as usual. *Why didn't you ride Charger back? Dad will ask. I got off to get some berries and Charger just went on without me.* Really, it was very simple. Peter felt so relieved he began to whistle.

He met his father driving down the river in the jeep. When his father saw him, he brought the jeep to a sudden stop. "Well, Peter?" was all he said.

"Want some blueberries, Dad?"

"Where have you been?"

"I—I j-just went for an early ride on Charger. I didn't think you'd mind."

"Charger came back without you."

"I know."

"Well? What happened?"

"He—I—the blueberries. I got off to—to pick some blueberries and—and he got tired of waiting, I guess, and—he went home without me." Peter shrugged his shoulders.

Jack studied his son for a minute. "Go on to the house," he finally said. "Your mother's worried." Jack turned the jeep around while Peter walked on. The boy felt strange. Instead of feeling better inside like he had expected, he felt awful.

"Hi, Sam. Hi, Mom." Peter tried to sound as if nothing was wrong. "Sure is nice out after the rain. I'm starved."

"Peter, where have you been?" He didn't like his mother's voice to sound that way.

"Riding Charger."

"Charger is not your horse, Peter. You have no right to take him whenever you want."

"Sam—" began Peter. He wanted to say "Sam doesn't care." But from the way Sam was looking at him, Peter knew Sam *did* care.

"Peter!" It was his father calling from outside. "Come here right away!"

Peter looked at his mother then hurried out. His father was standing inside the barn door. Charger had gone straight to his stall beside Old Nell's and was standing quietly.

"Don't you think you'd better take care of Charger?" asked his father.

"Yes, sure. Guess I'd better take care of him." Peter struggled to take the heavy saddle off and hang it up. Then the bridle.

"Rub him down. He's been running."

Peter did as he was told.

"Do you see anything different, Peter?"

"Anything different?"

"How did Charger cut his leg?"

"Oh, that's not a cut," Peter started to tell what had

happened, but he stopped himself.

"Not a cut? What is it then?"

"A scratch—a broken branch scratched him."

"That's a pretty deep and jagged scratch. You'd better put some medicine on it." Silently Jack watched as Peter poured the medicine on the horse's leg. "Give him some water, then come to breakfast."

Breakfast was quiet. No one felt much like talking. Peter caught Sam looking at him in a way that made him feel prickly.

Jack reached for his Bible as Alice cleared the table. "Our devotions this morning are going to be in the first chapter of 1 John. Peter, would you read the whole chapter for us?"

" 'What was from the beginning'—" Peter started out bravely. He had no trouble till he came to the eighth verse. " 'If we say we have no sin,' " he swallowed, " 'we are deceiving ourselves and the truth is not in us.' "

Verse nine. " 'If we con—confess our sins,' " he paused then began the verse again. " 'If we con—fess our sins, He is faith-ful and righteous to forgive—to forgive us our sins and to cleanse us from all un-unrighteousness.' "

He gripped the Bible tighter. " 'If we say we have not sinned, we make Him a liar, and His Word is not in us.' "

"What do those verses mean to you, Peter?" asked his father.

"If I've done something wrong or bad, if I've sinned, all I have to do is tell God about it."

"That's *all* you have to do?"

"Yes, sir. Tell God—and promise Him I won't ever do it again." Peter finished quickly.

"Hmm, and what does God do?" his father asked.

"He forgives me right away."

"Sam," Jack said, "what Peter has just said is true. When we do something we know is wrong, we must tell God about it. He will forgive us and help us to do what is right. But," and he looked at Peter, "when we take something of someone else's without permission, we must confess it to that person as well as to God."

Peter looked down at his plate. "I'm sorry I rode Charger this morning, Sam. I should've asked you."

"It's OK, Pete," said Sam.

"We'd better all ask God to forgive us for our mistakes," said Alice. After the "Amen" had been said to their morning prayer, she asked, "Jack, are you going to the Trading Center this afternoon?"

"Right. I want to pick up some new fencing. Where are you going, Peter?"

Peter was halfway out the door. "To the barn—to give Charger some more water."

"Maybe Sam would like to see his horse," Jack said.

"Hey, you're walking, Sam!" shouted Peter. Sam walked awkwardly to the door with a big grin on his face. He slowly eased himself down the steps and followed Peter to the barn.

"I'm going out to the garden," Jack said to Alice. He paused. "Are there any blueberry bushes on this side of the river?"

"No, not that I know of. Why?"

"I just wondered."

"Hi, Charger," Sam said, letting the horse nuzzle him. "Nice boy. Good fella."

Then Sam spotted the horse's cut leg. Charger pawed the barn floor as Sam stooped to get a better look. "Something cut you, boy. What was it?"

Charger snorted in answer.

"Pete, I saw you get up this morning."

"You—you saw me? You were asleep!"

"I woke up when you went out the bedroom door." He was silent a moment. "You were gone a long time." He looked again at Charger's leg. "Three hours or more."

"Was it that long?" said Peter lamely. His hand bumped his shirt pocket. He felt the bulge of his treasure still there. He had to get alone and look at it again.

"Aren't you s'posed to be doing the dishes?" Peter asked. "I'm going up in the loft and pitch some hay, then I'll turn the horses out."

Before Sam had time to answer, Peter scrambled up the ladder to the barn loft.

"I'll turn Charger out," called Sam. He picked up his horse's leg and looked at the cut again. He shook his head.

Peter waited till he knew Sam was out of the barn. Then kneeling by the open window, he took the old leather pouch out of his pocket and laid it on a grain sack so nothing would be lost. The stones looked small in the bright sun, small and hard and cold. Deep within himself, Peter knew he should show his treasure to his dad. Yet he still wanted to keep it a secret. Besides, if he showed his dad, he would have to tell him that he had gone to Golden Canyon.

But what about the gold? He had to know if the nuggets were worth fixing on cards for tourists to buy. He had an idea. Mr. Hunter at the Trading Center could tell him if tourists would buy them. And hadn't his dad said he was going there that afternoon? Peter put the gold back into the pouch and wrapped it in his handkerchief. He tucked it into his pocket, careful not to tear it more. Whistling, he climbed down the ladder and took Old Nell out to the pasture.

"It's a beautiful day, old girl," he said as he slapped her rump. Peter laughed as Old Nell ambled along. She joined Charger, who was already grazing under the apple tree.

In the house, Sam stood beside Alice at the sink, drying each dish. He was glad to be able to stand again and to help out with chores. But Sam was puzzled. "Is Peter still a child of God?" he asked.

"What do you mean?"

"His dad said he did something wrong, he called it a sin, so I just wondered. Is he still a child of God?"

"Oh, of course, Sam," Alice smiled at him. "We all do wrong things at one time or another, but God still loves us. Yes, Peter is still a child of God."

Sam said nothing. He would have to think this through later when he was alone. If you had to do *good* things to get to be God's child, how come you stayed His child when you did *bad* things? It just didn't make sense.

There was one thing Sam had to know now. "What did Peter do in the first place?"

"What do you mean?"

"What did he do that made him good enough to be a child of God?"

Suddenly Alice knew what had been going on in the boy's mind. She rested her hands on the edge of the sink and looked at him. "The only way you get to be a child of God is by believing in Jesus Christ and receiving Him as your personal Saviour. You don't have to do a thing! Oh, Sam, I didn't understand what you've been trying to get at."

"Can I be a child of God then?"

"Sam, do you believe in Jesus Christ as your personal Saviour? Will you accept Him now?"

"But I've done a lot of things I shouldn't," warned the boy.

"We all have, Sam. But Jesus makes it all right with God the Father. Now, do you accept Him?"

"Oh, yes, I sure do. Are you *sure* that's all I have to do? Is that all my mother did?"

"Yes, Sam, it's all your mother did, it's all Mr. Duffey did, it's all I did, and it's all Peter did. That's all you have to do!" Alice put an arm around the boy's shoulders and gave him a hug.

Sam stood quietly drying the same dish for several minutes looking at the table where he had worked so hard on the beans. He whispered, "All I have to do is believe."

Quite a Find

10

"All aboard, everybody. This jeep now leaving for the Trading Center!" Jack Duffey stood beside the jeep calling to his family.

Peter wrapped the worn pouch and its contents in a piece of paper sack and put it in his hip pocket. He picked up several of the cards with rocks glued to them that he had fixed the evening before and slipped them into his other hip pocket. Maybe Mr. Hunter would be interested.

Sam picked up the piece of ivory he had finished, looked at it, then laid it back down. He was sure Mr. Hunter would want it, but he wanted to give it to Peter's mother. Sam only had 67 cents to spend at the store, but that was all right.

Peter made himself comfortable on his knees in the back of the jeep so he wouldn't sit on his hip pockets.

Sam sat beside him. Neither boy spoke. They both watched the trees and fields speeding by and felt the fresh breeze on their faces. Jack pushed his hat back from his forehead. He was still puzzled over Peter's early morning ride on Charger.

Several campers were parked by Mr. Hunter's store and the green jeep pulled up along side of them. Two large trucks drove up the highway. A pickup coming from the north turned into the service station. The Trading Center was a busy place as usual. It made Peter feel good to be a part of it.

"I'll go over to the service station while you and the boys are in the store," Jack told his wife. "I won't be long."

Alice headed for the corner of the store where the bolts of cloth and dress patterns lay stacked on shelves. Peter knew his mother would be busy. So he slowly walked toward the counter where Mr. Hunter was talking to a man and woman.

A girl and boy were looking at souvenirs on the display table. Peter stopped at the table and began looking too.

"Hey, look," the girl gave the boy a poke. "Over there," she pointed. Peter looked too to see what was so interesting. Sam was slowly and awkwardly coming in the door.

"Look how funny he walks," whispered the girl loud enough so that Peter could hear.

"And look at his twisted arm," said the boy, staring at Sam. "They have kids like that even up here."

At that moment Sam turned to Peter. "Pete, come here."

Peter pretended not to hear. He panicked. How could he be friendly to someone who was being laughed at? Peter hid behind a rack of clothes. The boy and girl stared at Peter and then at Sam. Finally they looked at the souvenirs again.

Peter felt cold and then hot. He picked up a bright red plaid woolen shirt. But he wasn't looking at the shirt—he was thinking. He remembered the hurt he felt when Prince threw him off. He remembered too how it hurt when Sam laughed at his scrimshaw.

"Peter, what can I do for you? Do you like that shirt?" Mr. Hunter didn't give Peter a chance to answer. "That was a mighty brave thing you did at the fire—mighty brave. And you too, young fella." Mr. Hunter, with his arm around Peter's shoulders, walked over to Sam. Peter had no choice but to go with him.

"Sam, you were—well, that was really something. How's your foot? Is it OK now?" He looked at Sam's feet. The boy and girl forgot the souvenirs and went over to the candy counter.

"Sam, pick out anything you want from the candy counter. You deserve it—it's a gift from me. Go ahead while I see what Pete wants. Better tell these folks here about the fire and what you did. Pete, do you want that shirt?"

"N-no, sir." Peter glanced at his mother who was still looking at the dress patterns. He knew she had heard Mr. Hunter talking about the fire; he saw the smile on her face. "I—I have something to show you, Mr. Hunter. Would these be worth anything?" He pulled out the cards with the small rocks on them from his pocket.

Mr. Hunter looked them over. "They are nice, Pete. Yes, we just might be able to sell something like this."

Peter felt better now. "I have something else." Peter stepped a little closer to the rack of shirts. "These. Are these worth much?" He opened the piece of sack the pouch was wrapped in and showed Mr. Hunter his treasure.

The man took the stones into his own hand and stared. "What did your dad say about these?"

"I haven't shown them to him."

"Hmm. Where did you get these, Pete?"

"Oh, I found them. Honest. I found them in the woods." He looked over at his mother.

"Tell you what you do, Pete," Mr. Hunter said. He folded the pouch and nuggets into the paper and handed it back to Peter. "You show these nuggets to your parents and then we'll all talk about it. Now you come and get something from the candy counter too."

Peter walked out of the store with Sam. He smiled at the boy and girl who had heard Sam's "fire" story. Now they stared at Sam for a different reason. It was good being seen with Sam after all.

Peter thought about what Mr. Hunter had said. Before Mr. Hunter could sell the nuggets, Peter would have to show them to his parents. If he did that, he would have to tell about going into Golden Canyon and about the bear. And Peter knew his folks would punish him. But he had one other choice. He could put the pouch and the nuggets away for awhile and say nothing. In a few weeks, his trip to Golden Canyon wouldn't seem so bad to his parents.

Alice chose a dress pattern and some cloth. "I'll take three yards of this, Mr. Hunter," she said and waited for him to come measure it. "That was sure nice of you to treat the boys to candy. Thank you."

"They're nice boys, both of them. They sure were brave at the fire." Mr. Hunter shook his head as he cut the cloth. "That's quite a find Peter has," he said after a moment.

"Find?" asked Alice.

"Yes, quite a find. That'll be, let's see—three yards, plus the pattern—$20.50, Mrs. Duffey."

* * *

"You fellas all settled?" Jack checked the boys and packages piled in the back of the jeep before he started the engine. After they had gone several miles, both boys fell asleep.

Alice spoke softly to her husband. "Mr. Hunter said a strange thing, Jack."

"What did he say?"

"He said something about Peter having a 'find.' 'Peter has quite a find'—that's what he said. What do you think he meant?"

"Maybe the cards he fixed with rocks on them. He took some with him, I think."

"No, I think this is something else."

"Hmm," Jack said. "I'm sure he'll tell us if he's found something. Probably found something outside the store and gave it to Mr. Hunter. He just didn't think to mention it to us yet."

"That must be it."

Jack's thoughts were busy as he drove. What could Peter have found? Did it have anything to do with the cut on Charger's leg?

"Everybody out!" Jack called as they stopped in front of the Duffey's house. "Grab some packages, Pete, Sam. Peter—"

"I know, fill the woodbox!"

"That's my boy," said Jack as he moved the jeep to the shed. He took his purchases for the farm and put them in the shed. A small paper package still in the back of the jeep caught his eye. He picked it up. Maybe it was Sam's. Maybe there was ivory in it. Jack carried the package into the house without opening it.

"This belong to one of you boys?" Jack held the package in his hand as he went into the house. He half hoped Sam would claim it.

Peter put his hand on his hip pocket. The package must have fallen out while he was asleep. "It's mine, Dad."

Jack handed it to him without saying a word.

*   *   *

Sam woke up the next morning before Peter. He reached for the piece of scrimshaw under his pillow. The tiny flower he had etched on it was finished. The black ink showed every detail. Sam would have to glue a pin on the ivory so Mrs. Duffey could wear it.

Sam sat on the edge of the bed and examined his foot. The scar on the sole crept around to the top and it was still a bright red. It looked ugly and sore even though he was able to wear his shoe and sock. *It's ugly,* thought Sam, *but I can cover it.* He looked at his arm. *It's ugly too, and I can't always cover it. And I can't cover my crazy feet, the way they go.*

These thoughts were not new to Sam. He had thought them often during the hours he spent by himself at home. But since Sam had been at the Duffeys', he had come to think differently about himself. Maybe he really *was* like other people on the inside and that was all that mattered. Mrs. Duffey treated him like a real person— made him wash dishes and cut beans and sweep the floor. He had even stacked some kindling for Mr. Duffey.

Sam thought about Jesus Christ. Sam was glad he didn't have to do things to be a child of God. All he had to do was believe. And he was glad God had a plan for his life.

Mrs. Duffey had said, "God gives everyone the ability to do something well. And He gives His children a special gift called a spiritual gift. It is part of His plan for your life." Sam really did feel good about himself.

The boys were talking in the woodshed when the pickup drove into the yard.

"What does it mean to put off your old self?" Sam asked, thinking of the morning's Bible reading.

"I guess it means you aren't to be like you were before you were saved. You're supposed to be better. Supposed to be," Peter repeated for his own benefit.

"Oh," said Sam a little disappointed. He had hoped it meant he could get rid of his handicap. "Well," he tried to look at the bright side, "I s'pose it is important not to lie anymore and stuff like that."

"Yeah," Peter had started to answer. The words hurt him. He wasn't really lying—he just hadn't told his dad and mom *everything*. He had been trying to convince himself that he hadn't been lying, even though he knew deep down inside that he was. He started to defend himself when both boys heard the truck.

"Dad!" shouted Sam and dropped the piece of wood he was holding.

"Look at him!" said his father as he and Caleb got out of the truck. "He's as good as new." He rumpled Sam's hair. "How's the foot?" He looked at his son closely.

"I'm fine," grinned Sam. "Can I go home today?" Suddenly he was anxious to go. He had so many things to do at home.

"Sure thing. That's what we're here for, to take you home." Jesse walked over to where Jack was working. The two men talked as they walked toward the pasture.

"What are you two doing?" asked Caleb as he walked into the woodshed.

"Stacking wood!" said Sam proudly.

"*You're* stacking wood? Hey, that's great! Now I won't have to do it anymore." Caleb watched his younger brother prove his new skill.

"Sam, I brought you something." Caleb pulled a small red book out of his pocket. "I found this in with some of my things. It was our mother's."

Sam took the little book. Peter stopped working and looked over Sam's shoulder. "It's a Bible!" said Sam.

"A New Testament," Peter corrected.

"It's still a Bible," defended Sam. He looked inside the cover. "Maria Sealth, baptized January 14, 1960," was written there. The boy turned pages, stopping to read underlined words here and there. A small piece of paper fluttered to the ground. Picking it up, Peter read out loud. "Today Caleb Sealth made a profession of faith." It was dated August 12, 1967.

"That means you're a child of God too, doesn't it, Caleb?" asked Sam hopefully.

"I don't know. I kind of remember that day, listening to Mother tell about Jesus. I guess I did believe."

The two men were leading Charger out of the pasture. "Get the medicine, Peter," directed his father. "We'll put some more on Charger's leg."

Peter's heart skipped a beat. What if Charger got sick because of what he'd done? Jesse took the bottle from Peter and put the medicine on the horse's leg. "That's an ugly gash," he said. "Easy boy. Looks like a cougar or a bear could've done that."

Peter looked at the gash. It looked longer and deeper than he had thought. He kept his eyes on it as he said softly, "It was a bear—a grizzly. And she had cubs."

Sam Goes Home

11

The Sealths and the Duffeys sat around the kitchen table. In front of Peter's dad lay the empty miner's pouch, with the gold lying beside it. Peter had told his story, surprised at how easily it had come out. His mother and father had listened quietly as Peter told them everything.

"That is quite a find," Jesse Sealth broke the silence.

"That's what Mr. Hunter said," Alice smiled slightly, " 'quite a find.' "

"I wish, Peter," said his father, "that you had shown this to us first."

Peter bit his lip. He had wanted to surprise his folks with enough money to buy his own horse. He had wanted to deal with Mr. Hunter all by himself. But he knew he had disobeyed his father. He secretly hoped Mr. Hunter's approval would change his father's mind and make him overlook the disobedience.

"This is quite a find, yes—it is of value. How much I don't know for sure. Gold is selling for around $344 an ounce right now. We, you and mother and I, will take it to Mr. Hunter and talk to him about it. Then we'll decide what to do."

Peter looked at his father and then at the gold. He felt relieved at his father's words.

"What you did, Peter, was wrong. Taking Charger without asking was wrong and going into the canyon was wrong. Not telling me about the bear that got Charger and about the gold was wrong too. We all have to pay for the wrong we do. I forgive you and I know Sam forgives you, but you still have to be punished."

Peter glanced at Sam who was staring at the tablecloth.

"When we find out what this is worth," Jack went on, "you'll pay Sam a fair amount for the use of Charger. We will discuss the punishment for your disobedience later."

"Y—yes, sir," whispered Pete.

Jack wrapped the gold in the paper. "I'll put this in the safe, Peter."

"Now," said Alice, "let's have some sandwiches. You boys go out to the garden and get some lettuce and tomatoes. Sam, you can butter the bread. Peter, you can slice the tomatoes. We'll have some lunch here in no time."

Jesse Sealth watched Alice as she began to fix lunch. "I can't ever, ever tell you folks how grateful I am for all

you've done for Sam. You've shown him love, *real* love.
Most people are turned off. They don't ever get to know
him."

Alice smiled, then said, "We love Sam. Since we've
come to know God's love, we're anxious to show it to
everyone."

Jesse shifted in his chair. "You sound like my Maria.
That's the way she used to talk. But God can't love
everybody."

"Oh, but He does." Jack had been listening quietly,
but now he spoke. "I used to think that too Jesse, but
some folks who passed through here brought their
camper for me to fix. They told us about God's love. That
fellow had been accused of being a thief. But through
that he learned of God's love and forgiveness. He told us
all about it."

"But the things I've done! God couldn't love me. Why,
I've wished that Sam had never been born, then maybe
Maria—" Jesse couldn't go on.

Caleb studied the pattern on the kitchen floor. He
couldn't look at his dad now.

"You're not alone, Jesse," Jack spoke kindly. "Everyone has sinned. It's a wonder God didn't do away with
the whole human race, but instead He frees any man
who has faith in His Son. God makes it possible for
everyone to be forgiven. He forgives us as soon as we
believe and our sins are wiped out."

"Maria said she knew someday her prayers would be
answered." The big man felt tears filling his eyes.

"Make this the day, Jesse."

Jesse struck the table with his huge fist. "But I am a sinner!" He stared at his fist. "Lord, forgive me and make things right."

The two boys jerked open the screen door. They saw the grown-ups praying so they slipped quietly into the kitchen.

"Sam," said Alice after a few minutes, "your father is a Christian."

"Are you, Dad? Really?" Sam turned to his brother. "What about you? Are you one too?"

Caleb spoke for the first time. "I told our mother I believed in Jesus when I was five. But I haven't thought about it since."

"Do you believe now, Caleb?" asked Jack.

"Yes sir, I do," answered Caleb. "But I've done some pretty awful things too." His voice trailed off as he glanced at his father.

"God is our heavenly Father," explained Jack. "We have to obey Him. If we don't, He will punish us even though He forgives us."

"Sorta like you and me, huh Dad?" asked Peter.

Jack smiled. "I'm a father and God expects me, and mother too, to follow His pattern of how to be a parent."

"How in the world can we know what God expects us to do?" asked Jesse.

"The Bible—it's all in the Bible. Study it Jesse, and pray. Pray lots."

"Maybe," said Alice, "we can all get together once in a while for Bible study. Now let's get these sandwiches made."

* * *

"Well, Sam, get your things together and we'll head for home," Jesse said.

"Remember," said Alice, "Sam can do lots of things. He's slow, but let him try. Give him lots of opportunities and lots and lots of praise. He wants to succeed just like everybody else."

"I'm ready, Dad." Sam walked over to Alice. "Mrs. Duffey," he said shyly, "this is for you." He held out a small package wrapped in tissues.

"For me?" Alice unwrapped the gift carefully. "Oh, Sam," she said finally, "it is beautiful. Thank you so very much." She put her arm around the boy and hugged him.

"It still needs a pin on it." Sam showed her the back of the ivory.

"We'll fix that. Every time I wear it I'll think of you."

Peter looked at the pin and at Sam. The old piece of ivory he had given Sam was beautiful. Peter wished he could have done what Sam did. But he knew he had his own talents. He had never seen Sam look so happy.

"OK, let's go," said Jesse. "Do you want to ride Charger or go in the truck?"

"I'd like to ride with you, Dad."

Jesse gave a pleased little laugh. "OK, climb in. Caleb can ride Charger. Let's look at his leg again."

Peter held his breath. The cut didn't look any worse to him. "It's doing fine," said Jesse. "You boys could learn a lesson from that grizzly. She teaches her cubs what is dangerous, and she expects them to pay attention. If they don't, she slaps them or spanks them. They have to obey her or be killed by an enemy."

"Well," he held out his hand to Jack, "thanks again for everything. Drop by the mill and we'll look at those rigs."

"Will do," said Jack.

Peter watched the truck disappear around the curve by the dog kennels. Caleb followed on Charger. Suddenly the ranch seemed quiet and lonesome.

"Guess I'll miss him," Peter said to his mother.

"We'll see him again soon. Have you gathered the eggs yet today?"

The afternoon passed with its many chores. It wasn't till Peter smelled supper cooking that he remembered his father was going to tell him what his punishment would be. Whatever it was, he would not complain.

Peter took a long time doing the dishes. "Every night all by yourself for a week," his father had said. The longer it took, Peter reasoned, the shorter the evening would be—for he had to spend the rest of each evening in his room.

Peter went to his room and picked up his box of rocks. He dumped them in the middle of the extra bed and spread the cards out beside them. He had work to do.

Alice went quietly into her son's room. "What are you doing, Pete?"

"Fixing more cards," he said. "Mr. Hunter liked the others. You know, Mom, I've been thinking."

"Yes?"

"Remember how I hurt when I was laughed at—you

know, when Prince threw me at the picnic and when Sam laughed at my scrimshaw?"

"I remember."

"You said the Lord was trying to tell me something. I think I know what. He was trying to tell me how much Sam hurts when people laugh at him—so I could maybe keep them from laughing. At least stand beside him."

"I'm glad you see that, Pete, and I'm sure you're right."

"Some kids laughed at him yesterday at the Trading Center and—and I didn't really want to be seen with him 'cause I was afraid they'd laugh at me too. But Mr. Hunter helped me see how brave Sam really is and—well, I know how he feels when people laugh. He hurts, but he's really brave, Mom."

"He's not the only brave boy," said Alice. "I know another one who was brave enough to save his friend from two fires."

"Two fires?" asked Peter.

Alice smiled. "The fire of the forest and the fire of ridicule. This same boy is brave enough to take his punishment without complaining too."

Jack stood in the doorway. "We'll take that gold to Mr. Hunter next Thursday when your week's up. Pete. Now get a good night's sleep."

" 'Night, Dad. Dad, can I buy a horse?"

"We'll see, Son, we'll see."

Glossary

AMPHIBIAN PLANE: An airplane that can land and take off on either water or land.

ASPEN: A tree that grows in the north. Its leaves have saw-toothed edges.

BIRCH: This tree has graceful branches and oval, notched leaves. It is known for its white bark which is often used for making baskets.

BRIDLE: The headgear a horse wears. The bit (mouth-piece) and reins are joined to the bridle.

CASTORS: Wheels that are put on the legs of furniture so the furniture will roll.

CATERPILLAR: A very large tractor that is used on rough ground.

CEREBRAL PALSY: A person with cerebral palsy has an injury to his brain that causes some muscles of his body not to move as they should.

CHOPPER: Another name for a helicopter.

CINCH: A strong strap that fastens around a horse's body to keep a saddle in place.

DOWN-DRAFT: Air that is moving down toward the ground. A strong down-draft can be very dangerous to small airplanes.

ETCHED: Sam made or etched a picture by scratching with something sharp, like a nail or a knife.

FIREWEED: A tall plant with bright purple blossoms. It blooms in late summer in Alaska, making the hillsides and fields colorful.

GOLDENROD: A short plant with bright yellow or golden blossoms.

HANDICAP: A physical or mental problem that makes it hard to do things well.

HELICOPTER: An aircraft that can go straight up or down. It has long, narrow blades on top of it instead of wings.

HOLLYHOCKS: Very tall garden plants with flowers that bloom from the bottom of the stems upward.

KNEADING: Working or pressing something with your hands.

MUKLUKS: Boots made of animal hide, usually seal or walrus skin, with fur on the outside. Mukluks are worn in very cold weather.

PANSIES: Small garden plants, usually no more than 6 inches tall. They have flowers that look like happy, smiling faces. They are either white, yellow, blue, purple, brown, or a mixture of these colors.

RIDICULED: To be laughed at or made fun of by someone.

SCRIMSHAW: A picture made on a piece of ivory or bone by scratching with something sharp. (See ETCHED.) The scratches are colored by rubbing black ink on them.

SLUICE: A long, narrow box once used in gold mining. A sluice was open and slanted downward so that water could run through it easily. Small wooden bars were nailed across the bottom of the box. These bars caught the gold as the water washed the sand and dirt away. A salt called mercury made the gold heavy so it wouldn't wash away with the sand and dirt. A sluice could have many boxes joined end to end. Some sluices were as long as city blocks.

SMOKE JUMPERS: Men who fight fires by jumping from a helicopter or airplane. Their work is very dangerous because they often are surrounded by flames. Because of their special clothing, they are able to work closer to the flames than other fire fighters.

STILE: Steps that are built up one side of a fence and down the other.

TUMBLER: A rotating barrel or box used to polish small objects by whirling or shaking them.

WEASEL: A small, slender animal with gray or brown fur. The weasel can move quickly and get in and out of tight places when it hunts.